Queer Windows

Queer Windows: Volume 2 Summer

Copyright © 2024 by Cay Fletcher

Book and Cover Design by: Cay Fletcher
Edited by: Sam Fletcher-Taylor

ISBN: 978-1-959916-20-8 (paperback)
978-1-959916-21-5 (e-book)
First Edition 2024

Printed in the United States of America

Fox Fern Books, LLC

www.foxfernbooks.com

www.cayfletcher.com

Queer Windows

Volume 2 Summer

Cay Fletcher

Fox Fern Books, LLC

For all my Trans and Queer siblings needing the extra support right now.

You're loved.

You're valid.

You matter.

Keep fighting & resisting!

ALSO BY
CAY FLETCHER

ADULT FANTASY

Queer Windows: Volume 1 Spring

The Kingdom Asleep in Thorns

Masked

TTRPG JOURNALS

The Chronicle Diary

The Chronicle Diary: Pocket-Sized

The Ultimate Chronicle Diary

The Storyteller's Chronicle Diary

ANTHOLOGIES

"Sir Rexington's Bookshop", *Illusion*, Northwest
Independent Writers Association

CONTENTS

AUTHOR'S NOTE

Some of the stories included in this volume have content warnings. They are listed for each story below.

CAMP SPINYTOOTH

Mild fantasy violence.

A SILENT BALLAD

Ableism, descriptions of blood/injury, violent storms.

RIVER AT THE END

Death. Familial Loss.

STAR CHASER

Mentions of parental death and pet death.

FORWARD

As some friends already know, I wrote Queer Windows: Volume 1 Spring in a whirlwind of a few weeks. In contrast, Summer has dragged on for over two years. None of the stories have ended where I thought they would go. And all of them are far more personal than expected.

We're told to expect the unexpected, but in writing that can sometimes be frustrating. Each of the stories in this collection went through a massive transformation before arriving at their current form.

Queer Windows as a series is meant to explore different aspects of queer love and friendship. And give a snapshot of a queer normative world where being queer isn't a character's entire personality.

So emerse yourself in some magic. And I hope that you enjoy peering through the window at these little stories.

Cay Fletcher

In memory of Billy

CAMP
SPINYTOOTH

CAMP SPINYTOOTH

PENG & OPHIR

THE DEAD OF SUMMER wasn't supposed to be freezing. But, a freak thunderstorm in combination with the high desert the canyon was located in, had created a miserably cold, wet night. At least the streaks of lightning that painted the sky gave a moment of illumination to navigate by.

Peng wiped the rain from his goggles, clinging tighter to his saddle as a growl of thunder echoed against the canyon walls. He leaned forward, against the rain and ran his fingers over the smooth scales of Hopscotch's neck. The Grassland Green was panting as she clung to the rock wall with sharp claws.

A buzz sounded in Peng's ear and a tiny, pink heart icon began blinking in the corner of his goggle lenses. Tapping the side of them, the spell activated to connect their communicators.

"Peng, are you in position?" Rennie's rumbling voice crackled in his ear.

"Yeah, and soaking wet. Are we still all clear?"

"Yup. The patrols are all still on schedule."

Hopscotch trilled, staring through the murky dark at something the naked human eye couldn't see, "What is it, girl?"

Peng switched to the infrared setting by cycling through modes on his goggles. Three reddish-orange blobs came into view below them.

"Everything okay?"

"Shit!" Peng was already maneuvering Hopscotch into a better take-off position.

"Peng?"

"Gotta fly," he tapped off his communicator and nudged Hopscotch's sides. She folded in her wings and pushed off the side of the canyon putting them into a free fall. Even if his earpiece had still been connected to Rennie, the rush of wind and rain would have made it nearly impossible to hear her.

His heart found its place back in his chest when Hopscotch opened her wings, pulling them back upwards. The tip of one of her wings skimmed the surface of the overflowing river before they evened out again. Leaning forward so that he was nearly lying down, he tried to make out what the three riders ahead were on. Canyon patrol was usually done in pairs, with one councilor from each camp. Though he supposed they could be out with an extra pair of wings. Or they could be chasing someone.

The crack of lightning lit up the canyon ahead as Hopscotch twisted around a rocky outcropping. As they came around the bend, Peng squinted through the rain. They were going too fast for Peng to try and switch his goggles to another mode. The other riders had vanished. He didn't have time to wonder where they might have gone before the feeling of weightlessness overcame him and a spotlight shifted to focus on him, tangled in a near-invisible magical net. He knew Hopscotch would be long gone down the canyon, as dragon magic naturally allowed them to fly right through nets like the one currently holding him aloft, and upside-down.

"Camper, please identify yourself and your dragon," a stern voice said over a loudspeaker.

Lifting his goggles off, Peng sighed and tried unsuccessfully to right himself. Water streamed down his chin and into his nose.

The counselor with the loudspeaker came into view, draped in a bright orange rain slicker, "Oh, you're a Spinytooth kid."

"What's that supposed to mean?" Peng asked, trying to look unfazed in his compromised position.

"Hey, Voller! It's one of yours! You owe me drinks this weekend," the orange rain slicker councilor called out.

"Aw man," Voller dropped off their dragon's saddle and untangled their green hood from their horns. "I owe you two drinks. That's all."

"Whatever, he's yours, so you get to deal with the paperwork."

Tilting their head sideways, Voller peered at him, "Peng? Really?"

"Can you put me down now?"

Voller made an impatient gesture with their hands, releasing the spell and Peng crashed into the mud awkwardly.

"Let me guess, Rennie's also involved?"

"I'm not revealing anything," Peng grumbled as he tried to squeeze muddy water out of his jacket.

"Uh-huh. Look Peng, I don't get paid enough for this and I don't care if it's tradition to try to steal Umbertail's flag. It's still against the rules."

"It was just some friendly competition," Peng argued.

"In the middle of the night?"

"Of course. That's part of the tradition."

"Right. Well, starting tomorrow, you're on stable duty for the remainder of the summer."

"What? That's not fair!"

"It's perfectly fair. It's part of the tradition."

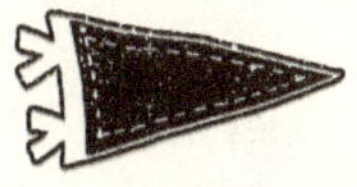

The stables wouldn't have been so bad if they hadn't been so stuffy from the storm and thus stench-filled. Peng had attempted to tie a bandanna over his nose, but it did little to alleviate the smell. Instead, he propped open the heavy doors on either side of the stables in hopes that a cross breeze might help with the odor.

Most of the dragons had been taken out on morning flights, so the only inhabitants left were the old, injured, and snappy ones. An ancient Mossy Green had draped her head over the side of her pen in hopes of scale scritches. Peng was desperately trying to scrape up all the muck from the floors rather than pay attention to the geriatric dragon. As he moved past her, she nabbed a tuft of Peng's dark hair, trying to chew on it.

"Honey Dew, come on. I have to get all this cleaned up before noon."

With a huff, Honey Dew used her front legs to prop herself up higher over the pen. Old World Greys had been specially bred for their friendliness and trainability. Unfortunately, Honey Dew was a drama queen who could never get enough attention.

"If you just pet her, she'll leave you alone."

Peng jumped, barely catching himself on the pen wall as his shovel clattered to the ground.

At least the interloper had the decency to offer Peng an apologetic smile, "Sorry, didn't mean to scare you."

"You didn't."

Honey Dew started chewing on his hair again.

"Right…"

"Do you need something?" he could

see the faded gray of an Umbertail camp shirt peeking out from under the other guy's flannel. Why the hell would an Umbertail camper be at their stables? It wasn't as if the two camps shared any facilities.

"Just to know where the tools are."

Crossing his arms, Peng wondered if this was the introduction to some prank, "Why?"

"So I can help with cleaning," came the incredulous response.

"Why would you want to help with cleaning *our* stables?"

"I don't want to help with it. I'm stuck on stable duty for the rest of the summer."

"I knew there were other riders out!" Peng proclaimed.

"Well yeah. It was the first stormy night of the summer."

"That's when Spinytooth runs Capture the flag. Not Umbertail."

The other boy looked around pointedly, "Pretty sure we're at Spinytooth."

"But your shirt…?"

He shrugged, "My parents sent me here this year."

"Why?"

"Something, something, I need to get out

of my shell. You know, parental reasons."

Honeydew head-butted Peng's shoulders in annoyance, sending him careening into the new boy.

The boy caught him, and Peng stammered, "He-hey! Honeydew! Enough!"

"Guess she likes you," the other boy said, pushing Peng away.

"She's a pain in the ass! No Honeydew, no treats today!" He turned to the dragon to hide how his cheeks were burning. In embarrassment of course.

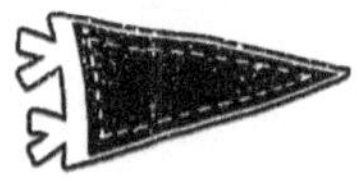

"He was probably the rudest person I've ever met, Rennie! Not to mention he comes from Umbertail. I bet he's here to spy on us. And I'm stuck with him for the rest of the summer? Ugh!" Peng collapsed onto his bunk in the cabin he'd been assigned to share with his best friend.

Rennie was wrapping a blue and pink tie-dyed handkerchief around her head carefully avoiding the twisted ogre horns protruding from her hairline, "Maybe he was just nervous?"

"Nervous!?" he sat up and leveled a glare

at Rennie.

She shrugged, holding up a set of golden bands that slipped over her horns, "Would these be too much?"

Peng huffed in annoyance, "You were born with the 'too much' gene. I doubt any amount of accessories would be too much for you."

"Well, I can't wear dangles during activities. Would the silver be better?"

"You're just ignoring my plight, aren't you?"

"I'm ignoring your complaining. Because it's not going to solve anything. You can stay prickly, or you can try to make the best of the situation."

He scrunched up his face, "Maybe I like being prickly."

"Or you just like being a pill. Now gold, or silver?"

"The gold always looks better," Peng said, having given up on trying to convince her that she didn't need to dress up for camp activities.

Rennie grinned and began slipping the bands onto her horns, adding matching bangles to her wrists.

"Are you going to wear that?" she asked, a tinge of revolution in her tone.

Leaning back on his bunk, Peng said, "Yeah, why?"

"It's the first campfire of the summer. You can't just wear an old T-shirt."

Peng grabbed a blue and green flannel from the end of his bunk and pulled it on, "This better?"

"You're hopeless."

"I try."

The screen door to the cabin creaked open and the boy from the stables stood silhouetted in the door frame, duffle slung over his shoulder.

"This is the Moss Cabin, right?" he asked.

"Oh, you must be Ophir!" Rennie said excitedly. "Voller said we had a new roomie for the summer by the way. Cliffside has a firebug infestation, so some people had to get shifted around."

Peng's mouth opened and closed a few times before he finally spat out, "And you didn't think to mention it?" Clearly the firebugs hadn't been *that* active given their new cabinmate looked scorch-free.

"Well, you were too busy complaining about stable duties."

Ophir raised an eyebrow, "I'm guessing the bunk by the door is mine?"

"Of course," Rennie said, going over to the bunk and picking up her bag that was open on it. "Sorry, we've had it to ourselves the last couple of years. So we kinda spread out. I'm Rennie, by the way. And this is Peng."

"We met," Peng and Ophir said in unison.

Rennie looked between the two of them and stifled a laugh, "You're the ex-Umbertail camper?"

Dropping his duffle on the end of the bed, Ophir simply answered, "Yup."

Rennie nudged Peng, "Your stuff Peng?"

Scooping up his pile of books and dragon magazines from their new bunkmate's bed, Peng dumped them unceremoniously on his bed across the cabin.

"Only rule is don't bug me when I have the curtain drawn," Rennie continued, pulling an old canvas tarp across the back part of the cabin to section off her bed.

"Sounds great," Ophir said, heading back out of the cabin.

Peng waited until Ophir was out of earshot before saying, "See? I told you!"

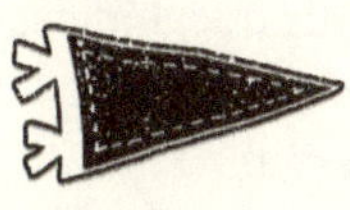

Ophir seemed to be around every corner. Peng had never had a problem with the dining hall table assignments. Or the logs around the nightly campfire being unofficially grouped by cabin. And worst of all, he seemed to be ignoring them. Which made being cabin mates with the newbie worse.

"He got up before sunrise again today," Peng said, watching as Ophir filed along in the breakfast line.

"Maybe he's just an early riser."

"Or he's spying for Umbertail."

"Why would he be spying for a camp he's not attending?" Rennie asked, exasperated, stabbing a slice of pancake.

"Camp loyalty?"

"That is ridiculous."

"Well, he probably still has friends there. Maybe he's the one that ratted us out?"

"We always run capture the flag on the first stormy night. It's not hard to predict there would be some Spinytooth campers out making an attempt."

Peng pushed his scrambled eggs around his plate, "He's still rude and suspicious."

"You haven't exactly been the most welcoming personality."

"I've been perfectly-" he cut himself off as Ophir set down his plate.

"Morning Ophir. You were up early," Rennie said. She'd been attempting to engage him during every meal, but had yet to be very successful.

"Hrm," he hummed, more interested in his food.

But Rennie pressed, "Are you going swimming today?"

"We have stable duty," Ophir said, glancing up at Peng.

"Ah, right. Well, maybe you can get some hiking in later?"

"I prefer riding."

"What'dya know, so does Peng. It's practically all he talks about. His aunt is a dragon racer, you know."

"I know. Do you want more orange juice?" Ophir asked, standing up to refill his glass.

"Um, sure. Thanks, Ophir." Rennie pushed her glass over to him.

Peng crossed his arms, "He doesn't know anything about me."

"Shush, he could hear you."

"Maybe I don't care if he can hear me."

"Don't be such a pill. And you better

shower after you're done with stable duty," Rennie said, getting up to clear her plate. "You stank worse than my brothers, yesterday." She followed after Ophir.

After pushing his food around on his plate for a few minutes, Peng finally cleared his plate and headed out to the stable. It was already sweltering, and Honeydew had been busy kicking up as much dust as possible. And chewing on her pen. According to his aunt, some dragon breeders gave particularly mouthy dragons diamonds to chew on. A camp like Spinytooth could never afford something like that though. Maybe lab-grown ones.

Hopscotch was snoozing in the loft of her coop, tail lazily twitching back and forth. A few Storm Crows had started roosting in the stable rafters crooned down at Peng as he started pulling tools from the supply closet.

"Yeah, are you all grumpy at me too this morning?"

"I already brought them some trail mix," Ophir said quietly in the doorway.

Peng jumped, dropping the shovel and pitchfork he was holding.

"Dragon tongues! You scared the shit out of me! Again."

"Sorry," Ophir said amusedly, grabbing another shovel. "I'll do these over here." He pointed to one half of the stable.

"Yeah, fine. I'll do the other half," Peng replied.

"Good."

"Good."

Peng caught himself glancing over at Ophir every once in a while. Making sure his cabin mate was actually working, not taking notes on their dragons or something else suspicious. It was nearly lunch when they'd finished mucking out the stables and feeding all the dragons. Voller had checked in on them a few times, before finally releasing them from their punishment.

"I guess you two can go and at least have fun this afternoon."

"What about riding?" Ophir asked.

"You're both still grounded. For another week or two."

"Come on Voller! It's not like I–we–did anything that hundreds of other campers haven't done."

"Maybe not. But you got caught. So here we are."

"Seems unfair," Ophir wiped the sweat from his forehead, pushing his hair up on end.

Peng realized he was staring at the sweat dripping down Ophir's neck and rolling down his shoulders. "Anyway, are we good for today?"

"Yeah, just put the tools away. And make sure you go shower before the lunch bell," Voller told them in a bored tone.

Ophir took Peng's tools and began putting them back in the supply closet.

"I can do that," Peng tried to protest, moving a water bucket out of the walkway.

"It's fine. Already done."

"Why do you keep getting up so early?"

"I'm trying to get familiar with the dragons," Ophir said, reaching out a hand for one of the Blues to sniff at.

"So you can report back to your Umbertail friends?"

Ophir sucked in a deep breath, "Look - you don't have to like me. But I'm not a spy."

"I didn't–"

"Rennie told me you think I'm only here to spy for them. I used to go to Umbertail. Now I'm here. That's it. Okay?" He hurried out of the barn without giving Peng a chance to attempt any more excuses. It left a pit churning in Peng's stomach.

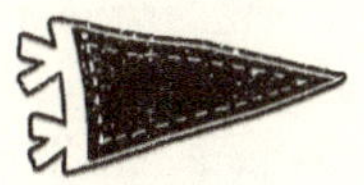

The lake was the only place to cool down during the heat of the afternoons aside from dragon riding. But seeing as he didn't have riding privileges at the moment, the lake it was. While Umbertail sported a huge pool and water slides, Spinytooth's lake had canoeing, swimming, and a couple of floating docks that were generally taken over by the older campers. Rennie had secured them a couple of floating rings and was drenching herself in sunscreen when Peng finally made it down to the lakeshore.

"There you are! You missed lunch." She held the sunscreen bottle out to him.

"Wasn't really hungry after shoveling shit all morning," he said with a shrug.

"Well, I've still got some snacks from home if you get hungry before dinner."

Spurting out far too much sunscreen on his hand, Peng started trying to rub it into his arms in vain.

"Hey Ophir, you need some?" Rennie called as she spotted their bunkmate.

Peng made eye contact with him, but quickly grabbed his ring and trudged into the murky water, "Meet you at the dock Rennie."

At least the water was moderately cool. Especially since his face felt like it was burning. He climbed into the inner tube and paddled his way towards one of the empty docks. A group of younger campers had claimed the closest one and were in the process of pushing each other off of it and chanting '*Sissie-Sissie!*' at the top of their lungs. The lake monster rarely showed herself during the day. But it didn't stop campers from goading her into sucking on the toes of their friends.

Bobbing up and down towards the dock, Peng could see Rennie talking with Ophir. Part of him wanted to know what they were talking about, but he doubted it was anything good. They had been their own, little pair for so many summers, and suddenly adding Ophir into the mix had completely changed their dynamic. He felt like Rennie hadn't spent as much time with him. Though being stuck on stable duty every morning didn't help. It's not like she was going to hang around the smelly dragon barn and chat while he did chores. She was just trying to be nice to Ophir. It wasn't as if she liked him. Rennie wasn't interested in guys like that. Besides, she had a dwarf back home she had a crush on.

Once he reached the dock, Peng tied his tube to the side and spread out on the weathered wood, an arm over his eyes to protect them from the sun. He tried to ignore the sounds of the other campers actually enjoying their afternoon and focus on the hum and buzz of the bugs darting over the lake.

The wooden platform dipped to one side as someone climbed on. "Took you long enough Rennie."

She didn't respond.

After a long silence, Peng propped himself up to see it was actually Ophir who had joined him. His legs were dangling in the lake, beads of water dripping down his shoulder blades as he sat on the edge of the dock. Peng could feel his face getting hot again as he scanned the lake and shore for Rennie. The sun glinted off of her golden horn bands as she lounged in one of the chairs on the beach with a group of girls from another cabin.

"Looks like you got ditched," Ophir said.

"She probably just didn't want to risk losing any of her jewelry. I keep telling her not to bother with wearing it here."

"Why? She likes wearing it. And she said that set was a gift from her friend."

"Girlfriend."

Ophir snuck a glance at Peng over his shoulder, "You don't have to be antagonistic just for the fun of it you know."

"I'm not."

"You are, actually."

"Then why did you bother coming out here if you don't want to be in my presence?"

"Rennie asked me to keep you company."

"I'm not a child!"

"Sure are acting like one."

Peng was about to retort with something witty when Ophir was pulled off the dock and into the lake. The other boy hadn't even yelled out, so for a moment Peng wondered if he'd slid off to swim back to shore. But then the surface of the lake was broken by Ophir trying to surface.

Diving in, Peng's fingers made contact with Sissie's slimy, eel-like skin. He tried yanking at her but was pushed away by a fin. The water was too silty to see much of anything, so Peng surfaced himself, trying to spot where Ophir was in the churning water.

Ophir's head came up for a second before he was pulled under again, and Peng swam as quickly as he could to him. He caught one of Ophir's thrashing limbs and held on as tightly as he could. Then he yanked hard and pulled his bunkmate back towards the wooden dock. At least Ophir was still conscious, and with a little help from Peng managed to scramble onto the platform, coughing out water.

Angrily, Peng grabbed one of the bright green pool noodles from where it was tied on the dock and chucked it into the water. Sissie rolled near it, her fins peeking out of the lake before she grabbed it and pulled it under.

"You could have drowned him you stupid lake monster!"

"*Dragon scales…*" Ophir said quietly as his coughing subsided.

Peng dropped to his knees next to him, "You okay?"

"Yeah. I will be," his brown eyes were red around the edges from the lake water. And Peng almost thought he might say something else, but Voller along with another counselor docked their canoe.

"You two alright?"

"We are," Ophir replied, a grin tugging at his lips as he met Peng's eyes.

Peng's heartbeat suddenly started echoing in his ears. Surely Voller and Ophir could hear it. But Voller simply held out a couple of towels,

"Why don't you both come back to shore and we'll have you checked out. Just in case."

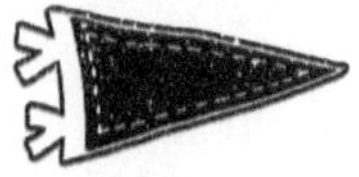

The near-death incident with Sissie at the lake had spooked a lot of the campers, making riding the much more popular option. Even though the camp's beast keeper had assured everyone that it was a freak accident, and unlikely to occur again. Mandatory life jackets were now being enforced.

Almost dying apparently didn't relieve Peng and Ophir of stable duties though. After another week, Voller finally took pity on them and put them back on the riding roster. Hopscotch was more than happy to be saddled up again as most of the other campers wanted to ride faster or more exotic dragons.

"Ready to get back out there girl?" Peng asked, scratching under her chin.

She chirped and nudged his shoulder.

Ophir was busy saddling up a sleek Blue that had been at the camp for several years. They hadn't really talked about what happened. Partially because Peng didn't want to bring it up if Ophir didn't want to. Even Rennie says that it's feeding into the cycle of not acknowledging it. He was up on his Blue dragon and nearly out of sight before Peng even got the all-clear for take off.

For the older campers, flight time was primarily used to scout out where the other camp might have hidden their flag. While they couldn't capture one during daylight hours, finding out where it was located was fair game. As he walked Hopscotch out to the take-off area, he did his best to keep his eyes off of Ophir. Though he was positive that the other boy kept stealing glances at him.

Pulling his goggles over his eyes, Peng ran through the final checks before tucking his knees against Hopscotch's torso and clicking his tongue so she knew it was alright to take off. She started into a gallop, her leathery, bright green wings pumping to get them airborne. Peng took a deep breath as the wind washed over his face and they began to climb higher. Over a week without riding had been near torture. Hopscotch seemed pleased to be back out as well, trilling as she spun them around in a barrel roll. Peng let out a whoop as she leveled back out, the tips of her wings just grazing the tree line.

"Hey!" Ophir's voice called out from

above him as Hopscotch soared lazily over the trees towards the canyon.

Peng shielded his eyes so he could see Ophir a bit better, "What?"

"Follow me!" he said without waiting for Peng to respond.

Hopscotch instinctively started to climb, eager to follow Ophir. Peng sighed and leaned into the saddle, letting her know it was okay. The Blue stayed ahead of them as they flew over the canyon and past many of the landmarks that Peng was familiar with. They weren't technically supposed to go beyond the canyon. But most of the counselors looked the other way for the older campers who had a better handle on riding.

A pair of peaks rose steadily in front of them, and rivers twisted in and out of view between the trees below. Ophir's Blue finally slowed and began descending, circling the ground near a grassy bluff. Peng figured Ophir wasn't taking him out to get ambushed by his former Umbertail campmates. Not this far out at least.

Slipping out of his saddle once they'd landed, Peng looked around the relatively plain hilltop. Sure there were some wildflowers and the distant sound of birds, but he wasn't sure why Ophir would want to come way out here.

"So…uh, what is this place?"

Ophir was unstrapping a bag from his saddle, "A place I like."

"To do what?"

"Just enjoy the day," Ophir said as if it was obvious. "Those two mountains over there are near where my grandparents used to live. I used to fly around all over here."

"Okay. Why'd you want me to come out here?"

Shrugging, Ophir sat down on the grass and leaned back against his dragon.

"Camp is the only time I'm really out in the woods and stuff."

"You live with your aunts, right? The dragon racers?"

"Only Aunt Lin is a racer. Auntie Briony is a nurse."

"Ah."

"Yeah."

"That's still pretty cool. I'm a big fan of Nightshade Racers. Though Ridgefield is my home club."

Peng frowned, "Ridgefield? I would never cheer for them, even if they were my home team. Their captain is an asshole. Always tries to cheat on the corners and cause accidents."

"Yeah, but would you cheer for another team when you're deep in Ridgefield territory?"

"Yes," Peng said defiantly.

Ophir chuckled.

"What's so funny?"

"You're just very cocky."

"I prefer assertive."

"Same thing." Pulling out a couple of sandwiches, Ophir tossed one to Peng, "Here."

After nearly dropping it, Peng sat down in the grass and started mindlessly munching on it. "Thanks."

Hopscotch headbutted his shoulder, so he tore off a piece for her to try.

"She really likes you," Ophir observed.

"A lot of people underestimate the more 'basic' breeds," he replied in between bites of peanut butter and jelly. "But she's a solid flyer. And all that extra power comes in handy. Blues are fine though."

Ophir snorted, "*Ceruleans* are especially bred for tricky terrain."

"That might be so, but they're also a lot lighter, so can't take an impact like a Mossy or a Grassland."

"Lighter means nimbler. You're the one that got caught in a net on your first attempt at

Umbertail's flag."

"You got caught too," Peng protested.

"Not like you did."

"Then how did they catch you?"

Ophir sighed, "Seabird here apparently can't resist eels. I guess the counselors had left some out as bait, and she flew right to them."

The Blue dragon perked up her head at the mention of her name.

"Yeah, it would have been great to know about you beforehand. I would have given you so many snacks you wouldn't have cared."

"You got caught because you chose a dragon that can't resist a snack?"

"It's not like I knew all that much about the dragons Spinytooth has before that. I've always flown on Ceruleans at home, so I just picked her 'cause I thought it would be easy to predict her movements."

Peng stifled a laugh, "I can't wait to tell Rennie that that's how you got in trouble!"

"Or you don't have to tell her."

"I tell Rennie everything."

Ophir's eyes flicked away from Peng, "Everything?"

"Well, she is my best friend. I mean you know how it is."

"I don't really have many friends back home."

"Oh, sorry."

"Don't be. I spend too much time riding for it to matter much."

"That doesn't mean you can't have friends. Do you belong to a riding club? That's how I meet new people."

"No. I just go out on my own usually," Ophir's gaze landed on the mountains in front of them.

"So you just go riding and go to school?"

"Yeah."

"Are you planning on becoming a racer or something?"

"Maybe. My parents are hoping I'll go into science or medicine though."

"You could always become a dragon specialist. Then you get the best of both worlds."

A smile tugged at Ophir's lips, "Maybe."

"We should probably plan the next flag run. And loop in Rennie, for communications."

"I think we did okay on our own."

"Yeah, but having Rennie in your ear does help."

"Are you sure the two of you aren't together?"

"Of course not! She's not even that into guys."

"And what about you? Do you like her?"

"I mean, as a friend, yeah…"

"But?"

"But what?"

"Is there someone else you like then? Or do you have a girlfriend back home?"

"No girlfriend."

Ophir's voice took on an almost hopeful tone, "Boyfriend?"

"No. Though I kinda wish I had one," he replied, immediately wishing he hadn't.

His cabinmate stared out at the sun painted landscape as a breeze played with their hair. Peng had never wished to be a mind reader, but he could see how useful it could be in situations like this. Ophir was impossible to read via non-magical means. Was he interested in him? Or Rennie? Maybe he liked both of them? Why couldn't he be better at understanding what people meant!?

"Thanks for saving me the other day."

"Yeah, no problem. Even if you're a spy, you would have done the same for me."

"Yeah."

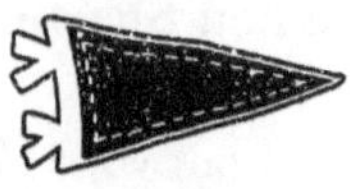

He woke up to the screen door banging in the wind. The latch had been broken for a couple of summers now. Since a prank gone awry by another cabin. Peng tried to ignore it, but it seemed like another storm was rolling in. He should have known when he'd seen the storm crows hanging around. They liked riding in on the storm fronts and then waiting for the winds to pick up to move on.

A shadow moved from Ophir's bed to the door, slipping outside and down the cabin steps. Peng rubbed his eyes blearily and put on his sandals and a flannel before following after him.

"What are you doing?" Peng hissed after Ophir.

Ophir paused on the path, "Don't follow me and you won't need to know."

"It's the middle of the night."

"Congratulations, you can read a clock."

"Yes I can, thank you." At least they were back to trading insults back and forth, it was better than the odd tension between them.

"Go back to bed."

Peng grabbed Ophir's sleeve, "Oh, and

leave you on your own to get into some sort of danger?"

"I'm much better in the sky than the water."

"You're still not familiar with taking off from our landing pad in the dark. Or all the landmarks. Or where our counselors hideout!"

Ophir covered Peng's mouth, pushing him up against a tree just off the path, and glanced around quickly before whispering, "Be quiet, otherwise you'll get us caught."

Peng's heart was pounding, and he wasn't sure it was from the threat of maybe getting into more trouble for a second time this summer. There was just enough moonlight coming through the quickly moving clouds to give Ophir's dark eyes an almost magical glint. The tension between them broke when Ophir removed his hand from Peng's mouth.

"If you must know, I'm going after Umbertail's flag."

The newly breaking storm was the perfect excuse to give it another try. Even Peng had to admit that. "Then I'm going with you."

"No."

Ducking out of Ophir's reach, Peng started down the path towards the stables, "Then come and stop me."

The other boy seemed to consider doing just that for a moment. But simply started after Peng, "Just...don't get caught again."

"Oh, don't worry, you'll be eating our scales," Peng taunted.

He jogged the rest of the way to the stables and slipped inside, making a beeline for Hopscotch's pen. A few of the dragons growled tiredly, but Hopscotch nipped playfully at his arm while he sorted out her tack. Ophir was saddling up Seabird. Peng would still take the sheer power of a Grassland Green over a Blue's lightweight frame any day. Or stormy night.

Before Peng could lead Hopscotch to the take-off track, Ophir grabbed his shoulder, "One run down the canyon. If we don't get it, then we'll try again during the next storm."

"Deal," Peng replied as the sky lit up with a lightning strike.

Hopscotch knew the drill—stay low until takeoff—then use the cloud cover until they reached the canyon. Given the failed first attempt of the summer, she was eager to be back in the sky.

"We're going to get that flag tonight, right girl?" He asked, scratching just behind her horns.

Leaning into the attention, Hopscotch preened.

"That's right. And we'll get it before Ophir has a chance."

Peng pressed his heels into her sides and Hopscotch lopped into a run, wings out. The air whooshing around them was the only sound Hopscotch made as they took flight. It was cooler up above the camp, the incoming rain was almost palpable. A burst of cold wind cut through Peng as a dark shape shot ahead of them.

"We're not having a repeat of the other night," Peng grumbled, bowing forward into the saddle until he could just barely see over the dragon's head. Hopscotch knew the way, driving through wind and rain was no issue for her.

Dropping down into the canyon, Peng nudged Hopscotch faster and harder, so they were whipping around the rocks and trees. He could see the blue up ahead. They would need to shoot up the shear wall at the end of the canyon to the rim where Umbertail's red and black flag waved.

A screech echoed against the striped sandstone. Competition always made it a little more fun. Umbertail had a whole team of Screeching Reds, and they usually used them to protect their flag. Spinytooth had always been a bit more lax about the game between the two camps and didn't do much to protect them.

Two dark blurs zoomed past Peng in the opposite direction. He hadn't thought to bring radios. Otherwise, he could have told Ophir to go guard the Spinytooth flag. Peng cursed under his breath as he pulled on Hopscotch's reins. If the other camp managed to capture their flag again they'd slip even farther behind in the rankings.

Puffing a cloud of smoke, Hopscotch reluctantly followed Peng's instruction to turn around and chase after the other dragons. She bounced between the canyon walls, gaining speed as they crisscrossed above the river. This year the worn pennant was hidden in a cavern tucked under the lip of the gorge. Peng hoped that the Umbertail campers hadn't discovered its location yet. It would buy him a little time.

The wind picked up, causing Hopscotch to teeter from side to side as she flew down the canyon. Peng was certain they must have been gaining ground as the rain began to patter against them. He shoved his hair out of his eyes and wished he'd grabbed something a little warmer. Or at least a pair of goggles. With water dribbling down his face, Peng relied on Hopscotch's better-tuned senses and reflexes to make it to the hidden cave.

One of the reds up ahead of them screeched and Hopscotch narrowly avoided colliding with the other dragon and its rider who were both tangled up in a net.

"It's okay girl, you got this," Peng said, though with the noise of the wind, it was unlikely the dragon heard him. His heart was beating just as loudly as her wings as they approached the final curve of sheer rock. A streak of lightning flashed, and Peng strained his eyes to see if the other rider had located the cave. But there was no sign of the other red. They could have easily overshot the location of Spinytooth's flag. Or missed the hiding place altogether.

Hopscotch picked up speed, flying straight for the tiny opening in the side of the canyon. A wave of heat hit them before Peng even saw the flames, and Hopscotch had time to adjust her trajectory. The dragon brought up one wing to shield him, liquid fire spilling over her scales before crashing into the rock. Her claws dug into the stone, perching them horizontally on the wall. Peng was doing all he could to cling to the saddle, praying that his harness held.

In retaliation, Hopscotch swiped her

barbed tail at the red and growled. Dragon fire was nothing to a dragon. Human riders, on the other hand, were fairly flammable.

"What the hell are you thinking?" Peng yelled at the other rider.

"Don't be so butt hurt. I'm just trying to win. What's a little friendly competition?" the Umbertail camper replied.

"Friendly?" Peng balked. "You could have killed me!"

"Oh, go cry on the phone to mommy!"

A wet splooshing sound was the only warning the Umbertail camper got before they were drenched with a blue dragon's slimy regurgitation. Peng could smell the putrid, fishy, odor even a few yards away. The other camper's screeching red didn't seem too pleased about the situation either, gagging and perching on a rocky outcropping.

Ophir leaned over his saddle and called down to Peng, "You alright?"

"Yeah." He could see Ophir's lips curled up to one side in a smirk.

Holding out a red and black flag, Ophir continued, "Good, we're even then. We have some celebrating to do, I think."

"You got it?"

"That was the plan."

"I'm reporting the two of you!" the Umbertail camper screamed.

Ophir shrugged, "I think the counselors would be very interested to know that you tried to scorch another camper."

"Yeah, I'd think again about trying to report us. Besides, we won this round. See ya'!" Peng nudged Hopscotch's sides and she took off back towards camp. As they circled the dragon stables to land, Peng could see clusters of flashlights down below. The other Spinytooth campers were eager to know if the attempt to capture Umbertail's flag had been successful. And as soon as the red and black pennant was visible in Ophir's hand the gathered campers and a couple of counselors burst into cheers.

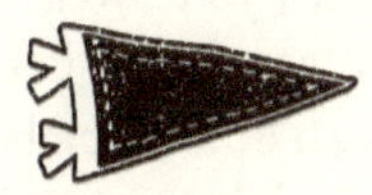

Rennie shouldered her way to Peng and Ophir's side through the throng at the impromptu bonfire, "There you two are! Why didn't you wake me up before you left?"

"My first night in Moss Cabin, you said you had trouble sleeping. I didn't want to ruin your beauty sleep since you'd finally fallen asleep." Ophir answered cheekily. "Or the two of you wanted all the glory to yourselves," Rennie jabbed.

"It was a spur of the moment, Ren. Besides, you would have had a heart attack when that asshole Umbertail rider tried to barbeque me."

She pressed her lips together tightly to give herself a moment to think about what she was going to say, "And how exactly does that make it any better that I wasn't there? I'm supposed to be on comms in case anything bad happens! Like nearly being turned into an overdone turkey! Can't the two of you *please* avoid any more life-threatening situations for the next week?"

"But…I wasn't?"

"You're lucky you two got the damn flag!"

"Yeah, we are, huh?" Peng's cheeks were starting to ache with how much he'd been smiling. Even though he hadn't been the one to actually *get the flag*, he was still going to take the glory for his part in it. Spinytooth had a flag and Umbertail didn't. The summer was starting out pretty well if their first failed attempt was ignored.

Rennie rolled her eyes, "Gods, why are boys so stupid?"

"We try hard at it," Ophir said, then wrapped an arm around Peng's shoulders, "We're gonna go get some snacks and drinks. Want any Rennie?"

"Yes."

Ophir steered them both out of the crowd, letting go of Peng once they were clear of their fellow campers. He kept walking along the path, passing a group of counselors who were watching the party.

"Hey, you two going back to bed?" Voller asked, always suspicious.

"No, just grabbing our jackets," Ophir replied.

"Alright, don't be too long."

Ophir nodded, motioning for Peng to keep following.

"Someone probably has a blanket if you're cold. Or you could just stand by the fire. Everyone would make room for you since you captured the flag," Peng said, once they were out of earshot of the adults.

"Are you going to be nice to me now that I did?"

"I–I…I mean…Is that why you went out tonight?"

"No."

"Then why did you?"

"Why don't you like me?"

"I do..."

"But?"

"But nothing! I just had some mixed feelings about you being an Umbertail, in the past."

Ophir stopped on the path, "Pretty childish to be hung up on a camp rivalry, don't you think?"

Peng stared down at his feet, "Yeah, I mean...sorry. I just haven't ever gotten along with Umbertail campers in the past. But I'm over that now."

"You are so annoying."

"Hey!"

"And loud."

"Look, I said I was sorry. You don't have to rub it in."

"And kinda cute."

"I am not–"

"You're not half bad as a rider either. Now that I've seen you up close a couple of times."

Peng swallowed, not sure if he'd just misheard Ophir, "Wait, what did you say before that?"

Ophir raised an eyebrow, "That you're

cute?"

"Uh huh…"

The other boy shrugged, "You are. I mean, if you're always this rude to everyone, it explains why you don't have a girlfriend or boyfriend."

They eyed each other for a long moment.

"So?" Peng asked.

"What?"

"Are we just gonna fight like this all summer?"

"We don't have to. You could stop being a jerk and just kiss me."

He blinked at Ophir, positive that his ears were playing tricks on him. "Excuse me?"

"You keep ogling me. I thought at first it was because you were jealous that Rennie was paying attention to me, but I'm pretty sure you'd rather be in her place."

"That isn't–I do not!"

Ophir smirked, "Then kissing me wouldn't be a big deal. Right?"

Peng chewed on his lip, knowing that Ophir was just trying to get a rise out of him. But his cabin mate was right, he'd been a little jealous of Rennie and Ophir getting close. He didn't know if it had graduated to anything beyond appreciating that Ophir wasn't half bad looking.

Though he wasn't Peng's usual type. He'd only had one crush, and that had been his math tutor. He tried to imagine Ophir with thick-framed glasses, and that just made his heart pound even harder.

Leaning forward, Peng pressed his lips against Ophir's. "There. No big deal."

Ophir looped an arm around Peng's waist before he could pull away, "That was hardly a real kiss."

"It was a kiss and it was–" He was cut off by Ophir kissing him. It was the type of kiss from movies where the love interest melted into the arms of the one they kept saying they weren't in love with. Ophir's tongue pressed against Peng's teeth, and Peng grabbed the collar of Ophir's shirt, pushing them off the path and against one of the fir trees. They were both breathing heavily when they broke apart.

"Happy?" Peng asked.

"Are you?" a grin was tugging at Ophir's lips.

"Shut up and kiss me again."

A silent ballad

A SILENT BALLAD

KYRUSE & NICO

★ ❋ ★

TWILIGHT LAPPED against the shore as the sea swallowed the sun, promising to return in a brilliant blaze on the other side of the world. As the stars peeked out from behind their inky veil, the only sound was the quiet ebb and flow of the water against the rocky beach. Kyruse had always wondered why the sea gave the sun back to the land each day. Surely the sea would benefit far more from its warmth.

Lifting their head just above the waterline, Kyruse scanned the shore for movement. Dark hair drifted around their shoulders like ribbons of seaweed as they bobbed up and down in the sun-warmed water. They had to be sure that there were no humans about before moving closer to the deep pools that dotted the craggy shore, filled with delicious morsels and snacks. The faintly rotten smell of algae baking in the late afternoon sun hung in the air with the lack of breeze to carry it away.

Stories sung by their pod—of humans hunting anything with fins and gills—kept most of the younger ones far from shore. The monsters of their epics carried spears and hooks and nets wherever they roamed, land or sea. Unlucky sirens, caught unawares by one, would be caught and strung up near their villages with the rest of the day's catch. A grim warning never to go above water without a song on their lips. But the nets the humans used and discarded were far more frightening to Kyruse than the humans themselves.

Kyruse had never seen humans near the tide pools. In their experience, the humans usually kept their distance from the rocky outcroppings and caves where the ballads of sirens lingered. But there was always the chance that one might get curious, or wander too close.

Glancing up and down the beach once

more, Kyruse spread out long strips of kelp over the large, flat rock that jutted out into the water. The tide pools lay a few yards inland, just far enough to allow the scales that covered Kyruse's tail and torso to dry out if they weren't careful. Seabirds picked at clams and hermit crabs while seals basked on every surface large enough for them to lay out on, paying Kyruse little attention. Mollusks and barnacles tended to cling to the areas of the rock that stayed covered by the surf. Which was why Kyruse always brought an armful of slimy kelp along, to prevent the sharp edges from gouging into their skin or ripping out a scale. Setting their basket out of the reach of the waves, they hauled themselves over the lip of the slab. Long, blade-shaped scales shifted in the evening light from red to purple as Kyruse's tail slipped from the water and they began pulling themselves across the rock.

The collection of dips and crevices that formed the tide pools caught the surf and a wide variety of sea life perfectly adept at living in the tiny ecosystems. They grinned over the first pool, catching glimpses of a field of bright turquoise anemones, arms swaying with the tide. Snails and crabs, sweet from how the sun warmed up the narrow basins, were by far Kyruse's favorites, but anything eaten from one of the tide pools was a forbidden treat.

Leaning over the first pool, long dark hair slipped over their shoulder and dipped into the water. Kyruse brushed their long fingers over one of the anemones, its arms sticking to their fingers before it closed up to protect itself. They pried an orange, spiny starfish, larger than their hand, from the side of the shaft and tossed it into their basket. Most of the pool's inhabitants spent their time scurrying along its walls, except for the larger snails; they preferred to eat the organisms living in the silt that collected at the bottom of the pool. Miniature crabs waved their claws in a display of aggression at Kyruse's invasion of their home. A few tiny sculpins and shrimp flitted into deeper cracks and hiding places that lined the edges as mollusks opened and closed to filter the tiniest of organisms from the salty water.

Reaching deep into the pool, Kyruse felt around for the conical shells of snails. As they strained their fingers towards the bottom, something sharp, like the jagged edge of a piece of coral, tore open a gash along Kyruse's arm. Yanking their arm back in pain and surprise, Kyruse watched as the water was stained dark with blood. It was bad enough that they weren't supposed to be so close to the beach alone, without getting cut on something in the pools.

Cradling the arm to their chest, Kyruse scowled at the rippled reflection on the surface, trying to spot what could have been the culprit.

A few stones bounced down the rocky cliffs that jutted up behind the tide pools and startled Kyruse out of their search for whatever had injured them. Something was moving on the foliage-covered bluff above, just out of sight. They had dealt with plenty of predators and dangers in the ocean, but out of their own environment, on land, was an entirely different game. There was no advantage on land from having a sleek, long tail, or finned forearms. And they were alone, with no other sirens around to start singing and lure an attacker away, or into a watery embrace.

Pushing themselves back towards the edge of the rock they were perched on, Kyruse's gaze stayed fixed on the darkening outline of the cliffs. It was difficult to make out the details amongst the shadowy shapes, but Kyruse felt eyes on them. If they could slip back into the surf then they could swim away to safety.

A sharp yelp pierced the usual babble of the beach and something large toppled from the top of the cliff. Kyruse crouched down, hugging the slick rock, hoping that whatever it was would lose track of them in its confusion. They held their breath, scales pulsing a darker color in a vain attempt at some camouflage. But it wasn't long until the thing stood and began moving towards the pools, making grunts of pain.

Even though Kyruse knew they should try to slip away before the creature moved closer, they were overcome with morbid curiosity. They had never been this close to such a large land dweller. Others in the pod often sang stories of huge, furry, quadrupedal animals that liked to chase things thrown into the water. But this thing walked upright, its steps echoing off the rocks. They wouldn't even be able to turn the encounter into a ditty to share with the pod, so Kyruse began to slip into the water.

"Wait!" the word was so dry and strained to Kyruse's ears that it took a moment for them to understand it.

The mysterious figure towered over them, and as it came closer, Kyruse could pick out some familiar features. A human was the only thing it could be, as humans were the only land creatures that shared a similar head and torso to sirens and other merfolk. Kyruse's scales and skin flushed bright red even as they were frozen by the impossibility of how close this human was. They had never expected a human to have just two legs, or be so large up close. There was a certain kinship the human shared with their kind, curly hair that framed sharp features, long lanky arms, and dark eyes that brimmed with concern. The sack-like covering it wore hid much of its body, Kyruse couldn't see if the human had scales or fins, or if the stories of them being completely smooth-skinned like an eel or dolphin were true. It didn't have anything in hand, but a weapon could have easily been hidden before Kyruse arrived.

Pointing out to the horizon, the human shook its head, "There are boats waiting."

Kyruse didn't want to take their eyes off the human, but stole a glance out to where the human was pointing. A school of lights were bobbing up and down on the water along the inlet to the bay. Boats meant nets, and while a properly sharpened shell could easily slice through them, Kyruse was especially wary of becoming tangled in one. The inlet was the only way in or out of the bay, and while there were caves and rock outcroppings to hide in, they dried up with the low tide.

They looked back up at the human, quickly assessing their options while doing their best to smother the growing panic burning in the back of their throat. Panicking led to hasty, deadly decisions. A siren only needed to make one bad decision to end up tangled in a net or displayed on a hook with the rest of a fisherman's catch. Staying near the tide pools would just lead to potentially getting stuck on the rocks as the tide retreated. Open water was safer in the dark, but if the boats didn't leave when the sun returned, then it was more likely that the humans would catch sight of them in the clear waters of the bay. And this human? Perhaps this human was just as malevolent as the ones laying in wait on their boats, a lure to keep them distracted.

Crouching down, the human peered through the dark at Kyruse, seemingly oblivious of the blood that was running down the side of its face.

"Are you hurt? There were some guys drinking and throwing their bottles down here," the human asked, reaching out toward Kyruse.

Kyruse turned their injured arm away from the human. It had started to throb along with their heartbeat and the drips of blood splashing against the slab of rock. They pulled their basket into their lap and fished out a strip of seaweed to wrap tightly around the wound on their arm, tucking the ends in to keep it in place. The human watched in fascination, inching closer. Kyruse flicked their tail at the human, careful to show off the long, serrated spine that protruded just above their darkly flushed fins.

Holding up its hands, the human backed off a few steps, "Sorry, I just wanted to make sure you were okay. I've never been so close to one of your kind. I've listened to all the stories though! Like how merfolk follow ships like dolphins. And about the sirens sent by Circe to call Odysseus' crew to the depths of the Aegean. Didn't they have wings in the poem? Or how selkie sometimes strip their skins off to live on land. Can you do that? Transform to walk on land? Or are you merfolk? How many species are there? Is species the right word? Or is family more appropriate?"

Kyruse gawked at the human. They had a distinct feeling that if allowed, this human would continue to ask silly questions unabashedly. Transform? Walk on land? The idea of traversing on land was an old fish tale, sung to unruly children when the movement of the waves wouldn't put them to sleep. That ancient art required magic that only the old patriarch, a sea god of sorts, possessed. Besides, it was dangerous, going to a land so strange and unfamiliar. Even if it did hold so many mysteries.

Letting out a huff through their nostrils, gills flaring, Kyruse slid closer to the water. Even with the boats closing off the bay, it was prudent to wait for the fishermen to leave while safely wrapped in the sea. Before disappearing into the water, Kyruse took the starfish from their basket and set it down on the rock, motioning to it. The human just blinked in confusion as Kyruse dove into the bay, relief washing over them as the surf passed through the gills on the right side of their throat. They glided through the open water, careful not to go far enough that they might swim into the boat's awaiting nets.

Back in the ocean, the high-pitched calls of their pod reached them. Kyruse knew from the tone that they'd be in trouble for swimming off alone. Again. Digging into their basket, Kyruse took out a pair of stones and clapped them together, hoping that the pod was close enough to hear the muffled sound. The reply was sharp and immediate. Unsurprisingly, the pod told them to stay put.

Sinking to the bottom of the bay, Kyruse flicked their tail at curious fish that swam by while they waited and gazed up through the black water, wishing their excursion hadn't been so rudely interrupted by the human. And yet, Kyruse wondered why the human had been so strange, so in opposition to everything in the old songs.

Kyruse took the admonishments and critiques of their pod mates with little care. They knew the pod had good intentions, insisting that they stay close to the protective wall of coral where the pod lived. But they didn't understand how mindless it was to be stuck with nothing but weaving or gathering to do, tide after tide. It wasn't as if Kyruse could participate in regular hunting or social situations, so finding other things to fill their time was something Kyruse was used to doing. Wandering out to the tide pools alone was too dangerous in the opinion of the pod, even though Kyruse was always careful to double and triple check for any danger.

Unable to vocalize their case, Kyruse's input on the situation was glossed over by the pod. No matter how much time had elapsed, the lack of support or desire to understand them was frustrating. Instead, Phorkys, the pod's de facto leader, had decided that Kyruse needed to be minded like a child. And Phorkys' decisions were not to be challenged. Even if the only thing that Kyruse couldn't do was call for help, or use their voice in an attempt to ward off a human's attack.

Laying between two hot vents, Kyruse watched the gas bubbles dart up towards the surface. Occasionally, a crab would wander over to the vent in search of shrimp or some other lunch. Kyruse would bat the crabs away with a flick of their tail if they wandered too close. A clipped tail was not something Kyruse wanted to deal with. Deino, their warden for the time being, sat weaving a basket, keeping half an eye on Kyruse to ensure they hadn't escaped being bored to death.

"Isn't there something you could be doing?" Deino asked them, twisting ropes of seaweed between her hands.

They didn't bother to sit up and just held up one hand, signaling 'no'.

"I'm sure there's something you could be helping repair."

Propping up on their elbows, Kyruse gave Deino an annoyed look. They'd spent the entire morning gathering kelp and braiding it into rope—for the very basket Deino was now weaving. Just because they were being punished didn't mean they shouldn't get free time. All their chores were completed, and Kyruse never left the few tasks the pod allowed them to do for long.

Deino sighed, continuing with her one-sided conversation, "You could be sharpening shells. That would keep you busy."

Kyruse opened their mouth to argue, a reflex they'd yet to thoroughly eliminate. But a muffled squeak came from their damaged vocal cords. They swallowed, running their fingers over the jagged scars that wrapped across their neck and throat.

"See, that's why everyone was worried when we couldn't find you. You can't trill or even whistle for help. Those rocks and shells you carry around with you are too low-toned for the sound to travel very far."

A few members of the pod who were working nearby had begun to whisper to each other, "They can't expect the pod to come to their rescue forever."

"Well, it wouldn't be an issue if they stopped going up to the surface."

"Phorkys should really do something about them."

"It's not as if they'd listen."

Kyruse ignored them, well aware of what the pod thought.

"What if one of those humans had seen you in the bay? You could have been caught up in a net again. And you might not have been lucky enough to escape this time," Deino continued. She had to realize eventually that Kyruse had heard all of this before. And surely would hear it again.

A human had warned Kyruse about the nets though. Not that they would attempt to explain that to the pod.

"You don't want to be a prized catch, drying out on a hook in the sun."

Their human had just asked a bunch of questions. It had seemed just as curious, as Kyruse had been.

"Humans have been killing us for centuries."

Kyruse's scales flushed red and they flicked their tail in annoyance. Their clumsy human could hardly stay upright. The idea of it with a spear or net, given the way it had tumbled down the cliff, was preposterous. It hardly seemed like the dangerous predator that the stories told of.

"Are you even listening, Kyruse?" The edge of annoyance underlying Deino's question.

The accusation bristled. Of course they'd

been listening. It was the only thing they could do, listen to the rest of the pod's complaints and songs and judgmental chastising.

Kicking up the silt and sand with their tail, Kyruse bolted towards the surface, ignoring Deino's calls for them to stop. The tips of Kyruse's fins flushed dark purple as anger filled them. It didn't seem to matter how many years it had been, or how much Kyruse tried to prove themself as a fully capable member of the group. The pod treated them like a child in need of protection, rather than a mature siren. When they reached the surface, the sea warmed from the sun high above, they wiped the water from their eyes and quickly looked around for any sign of boats before heading in the direction of the bay.

The tide was still in when they reached the shore, meaning the inhabitants of the tide pools might be out searching for food. Yet, as they bobbed low among the rocks, Kyruse spotted a familiar land dweller peering into the pools. It lingered, glancing around every so often as the surf washed up against its spindly legs. Kyruse wasn't sure if they were annoyed that their only refuge was occupied by a human. Even if it was their human.

Keeping just below the water, Kyruse

came right up to the large, flat rock, then popped their head up, squirting a stream of water from their mouth at the unsuspecting human.

Predictably, the human yelped and nearly tumbled over into one of the pools as Kyruse watched in amusement. If it was a hunter, it wasn't very good at it. The human spotted them and laughed, splashing Kyruse as they leaned against the rock, tail swirling behind them.

"I didn't think I'd ever see you again," the human said.

Kyruse shrugged, twirling a finger around a loose strand of seaweed floating by.

"I'm glad you're alright though. The fishermen were rather disappointed that they hadn't managed to catch anything while they were trawling for sardines last night. You didn't have anything to do with that, did you?"

Clicking their tongue, Kyruse pried an oval-shaped black clam, no larger than an elongated fingernail, from the edge of the rock. It came free with a faint popping sound, spitting bubbles between its bifold shells.

The human paused, waiting for a response that Kyruse couldn't give. They watched the confusion form, just like it did on the faces of sirens from outside the pod. Then the human's eyes wandered down Kyruse's neck, realization dawning once they saw the red, jagged, scars that spiraled around then down across their collarbone, and shoulder.

Biting at its lip, the human asked gently, "You can't speak?"

Kyruse pulled a hank of dark hair over their shoulder to hide the scar and pretended to be more interested in removing the rest of the clams from the rock. The small ones would pop like crunchy sea grapes. They could have retorted with something clever, if the human knew any signs.

Giving the human a critical eye, looking for any sign of weapons before slowly putting up one hand.

Mirroring Kyruse, the human held up their hand, "Does that mean something?"

Kyruse held up both hands and nodded, their tail moving back and forth to keep them above water. Then they dropped one hand and shook their head.

Grinning, the human held up both hands, "This means yes? And one hand means no?"

A smile tugged at Kyruse's lips. No one in the pod had been so quick to understand their attempts to find alternative ways to communicate.

Yet this stranger was grinning like a baby first learning to layer their gurgles with intention. It was odd how reassuring the human's actions seemed. The stories and ballads warned of lumbering giants more interested in killing on sight than engaging in conversation.

"What about letters? Or other words? Or your name?" the human asked excitedly.

Kyruse leaned forward and tilted their head to one side in confusion.

It didn't seem to bother the human though as they knelt and began digging through a bag before pulling a flat sheet of something out and unfolding it to show Kyruse. "Can you write?"

The human pinched the fingers of one hand together and formed loops in the air, "You know, writing?"

Kyruse shook their head, not certain what the human was talking about. The item they were holding out was curious though, with black markings covering it.

"I guess ink wouldn't really work underwater. Silly of me. Well, there has to be some way for you to tell me your name."

They had very little hope that the human would be able to guess their name, let alone sound it out properly, but it might be a fun game. At least so long as Kyruse could continue to slip away from the pod. A single human, this one at least, couldn't be too dangerous. It carried no weapons and hadn't been aggressive like Kyruse had been told humans would be.

Finding a rock to sit on that was just above the water level, the human leaned back, letting the wind pull at their hair. Kyruse plucked a plump starfish from the edge of the tide pool and used their elbow to crush it before starting to chew on one of the arms. When the human noticed, it gave Kyruse a horrified look.

"Those are poisonous!"

Kyruse swallowed and shook their head. Starfish were deliciously crunchy.

"Is that why you left the starfish for me? To eat."

Holding out the rest of the starfish to the human, Kyruse waited for it to come try the offering.

Instead, the human shook its head, "I'm good, thanks."

It pulled something from a bag slung over one shoulder, unwrapping a strange beige, spongy object. Kyruse had never had a sponge from land. They'd always assumed that they dried up outside of water. Besides, sponges didn't taste like much since they just filtered their food from the water. Unless the jelly texture that sponges had was appealing, most sirens passed them over.

"You've probably never had a sandwich, have you?"

Frowning, Kyruse wasn't so sure about how tasty a sand sponge would be. Especially coming from someone that wouldn't even try a starfish. But they held up one hand.

The human got up and knelt in front of Kyruse, holding the sandwich out to them. Kyruse hesitated for a moment, meeting the human's eyes and trying to determine if there was some kind of trick, before leaning forward and taking a bite. It was far softer than Kyruse was expecting. And dry and sticky. A large chunk stuck to the roof of Kyruse's mouth. They scraped their tongue across the sticky lump to try and dislodge it before spitting it out into the water.

"Not a fan of peanut butter and jelly then," the human said with a half-hearted laugh, staring off across the bay, the focus leaving its eyes.

Kyruse gave the human a dirty look as the sweet aftertaste lingered in their mouth. Maybe this human was just strange, because how could the majority like such things?

As the sea lapped gently at the rocks,

Kyruse realized that they hadn't felt so relaxed and at ease with another in a long time. Especially not their own kind. It could just be the loneliness wearing on them, making them susceptible to this human's kindness.

The wind whipped up suddenly, carrying a few notes of a mournful song along with it. Kyruse glanced around, trying to determine where it might be coming from, as the human looked off at the horizon blankly. A siren's ears weren't attuned for sound above water, but they suspected the pod was close by. They didn't have a chance to try to give the human a warning before hands wrapped around Kyruse, yanking them below the waves. Thrashing against the sirens holding them, the shallow water was quickly turned into a churning, foaming mess, as the human faded from Kyruse's view. No sound left Kyruse's lips as the other sirens pulled Kyruse, fighting at every flick of the fin, back to the pod's nesting grounds. Would a scream have even broken through the pod's melodic song to reach the human's ears?

Phorkys was waiting atop a throne pieced together from bits of ships and other discarded human debris. His dark red scales pulsated almost black. Two other siren's held Kyruse by their upper arms, keeping them from even attempting to sign.

"What were you doing, Kyruse?" Phorkys asked, his voice smooth as a new pearl.

Kyruse glared at the patriarch, shaking in frustration and anger, arms pinned to their sides.

Phorkys frowned after a long moment and waved away the others, "Release Kyruse, and leave us."

With just the two of them in the little hollow, the tension eased some, "You've been rebellious and reckless. I can't imagine that you aimed to put the pod in danger."

That hadn't been their goal at all, Kyruse had simply wanted someone, anyone, to spend more than a moment trying to understand them. Shaking their head, Kyruse avoided Phorkys' gaze.

"We all could do more to include you. I know that. Being angry can't change things, but I understand why you are. Losing something, a part of you, isn't easy," Phorkys said, raising the stump where a shiny red claw had been before being sliced off by a questing demigod.

Sighing, he pulled a string of pearls and coral from his neck and held it out to Kyruse, "Maybe you need a change of scenery? You aren't the first to feel out of place, and I'd rather you try to find somewhere you'd be happier than turning to sea foam."

Eying the necklace, Kyruse took it, examining the bright pearls and fiery coral for any clue or trick. They wouldn't be surprised if it allowed Phorkys to track them somehow.

Phorkys smiled, "It won't harm you. Go back up to shore and try it on. Just be aware, there is a cost."

Kyruse cocked their head to the side, questioning.

"You must tell me of your adventures."

Their hand went to their throat, fingertips tracing the long scar, wondering how Phorkys could be so obtuse as to forget they couldn't speak.

"You'll find a way to tell me. You're a smart one, Kyruse."

While questions filled Kyruse's mind, they didn't want to risk missing this chance. It was the first time someone had trusted them in so long. Kyruse would worry about the unknowns later. They were capable of finding a way.

Before Phorkys could alter his offer, Kyruse swam as quickly as they could, the necklace clutched in their hand.

Water flowed from the sky in rivulets as the ocean welled up to meet it. No lights were bobbing gently from above, as the storm seemed to have chased any sensible human far from the sea. Their human was nowhere in sight along the slick rocks around the tide pools when Kyruse reached them.

Pushing themself up onto the large flat rock, Kyruse shivered as the sky lit up with a bright yellow streak. A loud horn sounded across the bay, and Kyruse caught themself thinking that maybe this wasn't a good idea. If none of the humans were out, maybe it was too dangerous. They seemed scared of the raging storms that relentlessly crashed against the shore. But Kyruse wasn't going to allow a little rough water to scare them. Not when they were potentially so close to a new adventure.

Giving one last glance to the rolling waves, Kyruse slipped the necklace over their head. The change was slow at first, an uncomfortable tugging at their tail and fins and gills. Their coloration and scales began to fade and smooth into skin, leaving only the dark banding that wrapped their arms and torso. Clawing at their throat, gills began to close up and their tail split down the middle leaving two fleshy appendages. They clung to the rock tightly, knuckles white as the sea mercilessly clambered against Kyruse until the cold forced them to let go and pulled them back into the water.

Kyruse shot upright, gasping and sucking in air as the memory of the chaos of the dark water pulling them under into the bay came back to them. It took a moment for them to realize that they were in a strange place. Their body was twisted up in a sail or net of some kind with the only light coming from some human contraption that waxed and waned gently behind a transparent surface.

Every little creak and groan and hiss of the wind sounded horrendously loud in Kyruse's ears. And when they touched their neck to ensure the necklace was still there, they realized their gills had closed, leaving faint indentations where they'd once been. Panic began to bubble up in Kyruse's stomach and they startled, curling up as small as possible, as part of the chamber opened to reveal the dark-haired human from the beach.

It smiled as they set down a tray, "I'm glad you woke up. I was worried you might not. I brought some water. And cured fish. I didn't know if you'd be hungry or not."

Relaxing a little, Kyruse looked around the chamber again. The walls were cool and smooth, like the rocks by the shoreline. It didn't seem nearly as scary now that the human had appeared.

Prattling on, the human started moving things around, "I cleaned up the cuts you had. But the bruises will probably ache for a while. Especially the ribs. I didn't really think that your kind could grow legs. Though I guess there's that fairytale. Are sea witches real then?"

Kyruse frowned and tried to untangle themselves from the sail at the mention of legs. Pulling at the rest of the coverings wrapped around their limbs, they weren't certain if the lump they felt forming in the back of their throat was excitement or dread.

The human's face started turning red, "Oh, let me help! I uh…I figured clothes might be a good idea. It's generally best to wear them if you don't want people to think you're odd. Not that it's the only reason someone might think you're odd," the human easily pulled the sail away, revealing wriggling toes, two feet, and a pair of legs where Kyruse's fins and tail had been.

They just stared for a long moment, getting used to the sensation of toes rather than fins. Their new appendages were a sandy color, with darker banding spiraling up. Though the legs lacked their scales reds and purples and the way their coloration would shift and ripple with their mood. Were all human limbs truly this boring? They leaned forward, ignoring the pain that bloomed up their side, and brushed newly webless fingers over long, scrunched-up toes.

"Is it weird having legs instead of a tail?" the human asked.

Lifting one leg, then the other, Kyruse tried to get used to the motion. It was nothing like what they were used to. Legs weren't nearly as flexible and only wanted to bend in certain ways.

Holding out its hand, the human smiled again, "Do you want some help?"

They weren't sure what kind of help the human could offer. Learning to use the new parts of their body wasn't exactly a task that could be shared. But Kyruse took the human's hand, surprised by how steady it was. Shifting, the human carefully hooked an arm under Kyruse's armpits, gently supporting them, taking their weight, and moving slowly as Kyruse moved their feet to the wooden floor. They curled up their toes instinctively after their feet settled on the chilly planks. The extremes of hot and cold were intense, a fault of a human's thin, mostly hairless skin. Trying to balance without the ocean's embrace was another new sensation. Kyruse found themselves holding their arms out to their sides, mimicking a crab's walk, in some vain, instinctual, attempt not to fall over. At even the faintest wobble, the human's arms were there to catch them. Wrapped gently around their torso, careful to avoid every bandaged injury.

"You're standing! Now hold on," the human shifted to stand in front of Kyruse, gripping their elbows.

There was a moment that Kyruse's legs shuddered, but the human's grip kept them from falling, "Don't worry, I've got you."

Dark eyes locked on each other, and the human carefully guided Kyruse's first steps. It was more shuffling than walking at first, with Kyruse unable to lift their feet to take a proper step. The human picked them up from their first fall. And laughed alongside them when they managed to twirl across the room on their own. The sun's morning rays were peeking through a crack in the draperies before they'd both thoroughly exhausted themselves and collapsed again, Kyruse laying their head in the human's lap.

Kyruse felt the tug of a smile at their lips and turned to the human. They couldn't remember the last time they'd felt so accomplished. Since losing their voice it had felt like every day brought a new opportunity for failure.

"We should probably get some sleep. You do sleep, right?"

Kyruse rolled their eyes, then tapped their collarbone, mimicking the gesture against the human's collarbone. They realized they didn't know if the human had a name. It had asked about theirs, but Kyruse didn't have any way to tell them.

The human looked down at them puzzled for a moment, "You…or me?"

Tapping the human's collarbone again, Kyruse held up both hands, yes.

"Me?" It thought for a long moment, leaning back on its hands, "Oh! Do you mean my name?"

Kyruse nodded enthusiastically.

"I'm Nico. How do you communicate with the others? Maybe we could try that?"

The thought of trying to teach the human, Nico, the few words the pod had managed to learn from Kyruse clapping together two rocks just brought on a wave of dread. It hadn't worked with them, so why would a human be able to learn? Shaking their head, Kyruse moved to sit up.

Nico put an arm across Kyruse's chest,

gently preventing them from moving, "I'm willing to learn. I know I talk a lot, but you must have things you want to say. And I already know yes and no, and now," he tapped his collarbone, "Me and you. We can do it together."

Kyruse had never felt the sensation of tears before. They touched the salty trails left in their wake and smiled. The tales the elders told always made it sound like crying was a sad affair with tears turning to pearls. But Kyruse couldn't have been happier. A stranger, a human, the thing they were supposed to fear and stay away from, was offering something their own blood never had.

Understanding.

Rounding the spiral stairs up to the very top of the lighthouse, Kyruse collapsed against the railings, chest heaving as their breath caught up to their excitement. Nico offered them a hand up and pulled them over to the little couch that someone had hauled up to the sitting area just below the light room. The dizzy feeling that Kyruse got from running as fast as they could up the steps was addictive. Especially when Nico was waiting up at the top for them. Kyruse curled up, half in Nico's lap as their heartbeat thundered in their ears. Weeks or months had gone by, and Kyruse had used every moment to be as close to Nico as possible.

"You're never going to get tired of that, are you?" Nico asked, running his fingers through Kyruse's long, silky hair.

Kyruse shook their head and leaned into the touch. They'd never known how much they liked to be touched before. Skin against skin was so much more pleasant than scales and fins. And Nico was always warm like a shallow pool of water on a sunny day. Curling their toes against the arm of the couch and closing their eyes, Kyruse pinched their fingers together and moved them against their mouth.

"No, I can wait until dinner. Are you hungry?" Nico responded. The two of them had already developed hundreds of signs going hours without speaking a word to each other. It wasn't a perfect system, and there were still moments of frustration and misunderstanding. But they felt so in sync, almost as if they could sing the same tune without needing to know the words. Kyruse couldn't be happier.

Opening one eye, Kyruse shrugged.

Nico laughed, "There are only a couple hours till dinner. And if you help me clean the glass it'll go faster."

Tapping their chin as if thinking it over, Kyruse finally nodded in agreement and got to their feet. The one part they disliked about the lighthouse was how high up it was. They'd never been afraid of swimming over even the deepest trenches, but going out to the walkway that surrounded the lighthouse's lamp terrified Kyruse. Staying inside the safety of the lightroom at least gave some feeling of assurance.

It was a beautiful view though, standing at what felt like the top of the world looking out beyond the horizon as it curved away. As they climbed the last twenty-one steps up to the lightroom Kyruse looked out to the clouds that were lying in wait, heavy with rain. The bright blue of the afternoon was quickly fading, and Kyruse could feel the dread building in the pit of their stomach. Seeing a storm from above in the lightroom was very different from drifting through the rolling waves beneath the surface.

They turned to Nico and pointed at the clouds before twirling two fingers in a circle.

"Don't worry, we'll be quick. It's still a

ways off," Nico squeezed Kyruse's hand gently and smiled again. He knew exactly how to smooth Kyruse's nerves and set them back at ease. Picking up one of the buckets of soapy water and the stiff-bristled broom, Nico slipped out to the gallery to wash the windows.

Kyruse had taken over the job of polishing the intricate lens of the lamp. Nico had explained it was especially important during storms for the lighthouse to be in top condition so ships didn't wreck on the rocks near the entrance to the bay. His family had been guardians of this coastline for generations. Nico had slowly been taking over its care as his relatives aged and could no longer scale the hundreds of steps every day.

Using a rag, they carefully dusted every nook and cranny of the sheets of glass. Their narrow, slender fingers were ideal for it, just like reaching into the crooks of rocks or coral searching for snacks. They had to be careful not to touch or scratch any of the delicate glass panels as it would affect how the light traveled across the landscape.

The lilt of Nico's voice carried through the lightroom as he worked. It wasn't polished or pretty, and Kyruse was sure that half the time Nico simply made up the words, but it was comforting to hear as the wind whipped up.

When Nico came back inside, he was half drenched from the wind blowing his cleaning water around. Kyruse grabbed a blanket that was folded over the railing and wrapped it around Nico's shoulders, frowning at Nico's carelessness. They dabbed up drops of water and soap from Nico's fluffy curls so that he wouldn't catch the chill that humans seemed to dread. To his credit, Nico allowed Kyruse's fussing as the first of the rain began to patter against the lightroom's curved, glass panes.

"Do you want to light it while I make sure the clockwork is wound?"

Kyruse had watched Nico light the lamp every night, a bit wary of the flickering flame used to bring it to life every evening. But they nodded, taking the long-handled lighter from Nico. Their human friend lingered at the top of the stairs for a moment before offering another reassuring smile and going down below to inspect the clockwork that ensured the lamp spun throughout the night. Lifting the latch on one side of the lens, Kyruse opened it and leaned over towards the wick. They clicked the trigger on the lighter a few times until the flame was steady and then touched it to the wick so the fire hopped from the lighter.

With the lamp lit, Kyruse carefully closed the lens again. The yellow glow was beautiful as it filtered through the facets of the lens. It reminded them of the way the sun would reach down through the waves, breaking into shafts of light. They stepped back to admire their work, then went back with the cloth to wipe away a few final smudges.

"All ready up there?" Nico called.

Going over to the stair rail, Kyruse looked down and held up both hands to him.

Disappearing again for a moment, Nico pulled back the leaver and locked it into place as the gears creaked into motion. Slowly, the lamp began to turn, broadcasting bright white light out into the stormy weather. Kyruse covered their ears as the deep rumble of the foghorn bellowed. Human ears were so much more sensitive on land, which Kyruse had learned after standing too close to the horn the first time they'd gone up to the light room with Nico. Luckily it wasn't used very often, except to indicate that the lamp was lit, or was being put out for the day.

Soup and crab cakes and little morsels of fried fish were dropped off at the lighthouse's tiny cottage by Nico's grandmother. Their tastes had quickly shifted to more human fare, though with a fair helping of extra salt. Dried seaweed and kelp, seasoned with Nico's grandmother's secret mixture of spices had quickly become their favorite thing. They curled up on the couch to eat as the sky flushed wine red and to watch as the storm came in.

As it howled around them, Nico wrapped his arms around Kyruse's waist, pulling them closer, "Are you ever going to go back?"

Kyruse's fingers twisted in the necklace of pearls and coral. It wasn't the first time Nico had asked and Kyruse couldn't answer. Phorkys hadn't told them to come back, but there had been an implication that someday they'd have to return. They had no idea how long the magic would work. Or if Nico would grow wrinkled and old, bent over a cane like so many of the townsfolk, while they stayed much the same. There were still parts of them that weren't fully human, and Kyruse didn't know if those would start to fade the longer they stayed on land or if they'd always be a mix of the two.

They nuzzled their head under Nico's chin, and Nico didn't ask again. Instead, he pulled a thin, silver instrument from his jacket and held it out for Kyruse to see.

"This was my grandfather's flute, I thought

you might want to try it," Nico said, putting the instrument to his lips and blowing through it. The notes rang clear and cheerful in contrast to the wind's bluster. He handed it to Kyruse, showing them how to balance the instrument delicately with their fingers. And how to form the correct mouth shape so the sound would come out strong.

Some of the town's people had whistles or other similar instruments, but the sounds they produced were harsh. Meant for warnings and commands rather than the gentle lure of a song. Kyruse mimicked the way Nico had held it to his lips and blew a few times, adjusting their fingers over the holes until it produced the note they wanted. They slowly pieced together individual notes into a song they used to sing to guide schools of fish along the path of a current. Nico seemed pleased that they enjoyed it so much, almost as if a little bit of a siren's song was able to come through in Kyruse's playing.

Getting to their feet, Kyruse rushed up to the lightroom, a thought dawning on them. Nico called after them, but his voice was drowned out by the wind and rain as Kyruse opened the door to the gallery.

The cold cut through the clothes they were wearing, and rain dripped down their face, but as Kyruse put the flute to their lips again and began to play they could feel the primal call that all sirens layered into their songs. They weren't sure how, but they knew that the song would reach Phorkys and the rest of the pod where they were probably relaxing in the pleasant tumbling of the waves. It wasn't a mournful song of loss or meant to beckon anyone to a watery grave. The ballad was a declaration, raw and full of every emotion that had bubbled inside for too long, unable to be put into words.

They didn't finish until the clouds drifted away and the soft gray light of morning crept up from behind the hills. And Nico was there, with happy tears and a smile to take Kyruse's shaking hands in his and wrap a warm blanket around their shoulders.

Fins or feet, song or signs, they knew this was the brave new adventure they wanted to take on.

river at
the end

Cay Fletcher

RIVER AT THE END

AYSEL

MANY THOUGHT IT WAS a simple thing to walk through a portal to another world. Navigating the tangle of interconnected passages within the network of otherworlds took either a great amount of skill and practice, or a good deal of reckless abandon. Aysel wasn't certain which of those qualities she inhabited. Breezing through the spaces between realities had always been a part of her life as she tagged along with her grandmother on errands and visits to old friends.

Bag slung over her shoulder, Aysel nudged the edge of the sewer cover with her foot.

It was one of the few permanent entrances left, the years having worn away at the magic keeping the portal active. Fewer portals did mean fewer people accidentally wandering into places they shouldn't be. But disappearing into a sewer was more conspiracies than she'd like.

Kneeling, Aysel pulled out the chalk she kept in a pouch clipped to the strap of her bag and drew a circle around the sewer cover, scribbling the symbols her grandmother had taught her around it. There was a faint flash of golden light and she grinned as she hooked a finger into one of the holes, lifting up the cover. The heavy metal grated against the pavement, the sound echoing against the quiet buildings. Before any busybodies nearby could pop their head out a window to see what was going on, Aysel pulled her hood up and jumped into the sewer-turned-portal, letting the warm air, entrenched in the smells of street food wash over her.

This first portal was always a little like floating until her feet touched the stone street, she walked through an ancient archway, covered in climbing plants, and into a vibrant and lively marketplace. Being the first place her grandmother had taken her, the busy streets held a special place in her heart. Golden lanterns at the tops of wooden posts cast shadows that crisscrossed the narrow alleyways along with strings of colorful flags and kites. The streets were always packed with people here, so Aysel held her bag in front of her as she tried to navigate through the throng of shoppers.

As the crowd lagged momentarily, she paused in front of one stall selling floating goldfish, bobbing gently against each other on their little leashes of red thread. One of the fish swam in her direction and tried to get tangled in the straps of her bag.

The merchant, draped in water-printed silk, caught her eye, "Interested in one, sweetie?"

"Oh, I've got a long way home and I just started my evening," Aysel glanced at her watch, glad that she hadn't lost too much time yet.

"They're lovely pets," the merchant said, a grin spreading across her face as she stroked the dorsal fin of one of the goldfish. Its scales flushed through a rainbow of colors as it nuzzled her fingers. "Very easy to keep."

"My partner would kill me if I brought another pet home. But thanks!"

"You should bring your partner next time," the seller purred, her pupils contracting to narrow slits.

Aysel laughed uncomfortably, giving a noncommittal response. There were too many risks in agreeing to anything while traversing one of the otherworlds. More so when a merchant's voice could lay in a contract unbeknownst to the traveler.

Slipping back into the flow of shoppers, Aysel kept an eye out for the lantern stall, barely resisting the numerous, delicious-smelling treats being held out by enthusiastic stall owners. Skewers of sweet and spicy roasted meat. Iced drinks. Traditional bean paste candies. Fried bread, or potatoes, or vegetables. Her mouth was watering as she let the crowd guide her through the street. She normally tried to remember to eat before going off on a trip through the otherworlds, but she'd been in a bit of a hurry that night. Her partner had packed her dinner, the last thing she needed was to succumb to the temptation of eating food from another world, only to end up stuck there.

A clear chime of some instrument rang through the air and the crowd parted to reveal a parade of revelers holding lanterns. It reminded Aysel to look at her watch again. Almost an hour had passed since she jumped down the manhole. Even if it didn't feel like that much time had passed, Aysel knew the timepiece was accurate, her grandfather had ensured that it would always give her the correct reading.

The revelers wore stylized masks of animals, spirits, and demons, but in the lantern light, she could see their fur-covered hands, scales, or flesh unlike any human had. Strange lights followed alongside the parade, dipping and rising as the line of locals wound through the crowd. Pressing her back against the corner of a stall, Aysel watched the procession in fascination. She'd always wished she could join them, but as her grandmother had explained, some things were just not for them. They could observe, but participating was out of the question.

As the parade petered out, Aysel melted back into the ebb and flow of shoppers, until she finally spotted the lantern stall. Delicate paper creations were hung from every surface of the tiny, barely held together structure and glowed a welcoming golden color. The old man who ran the stall gave her a once over before commenting, "It's that time is it?"

"It is. I almost thought I wouldn't find your stall."

"Yet here you are," he replied.

"She always brags that your lanterns are

the best."

He didn't respond, instead, taking down a simple white cylindrical lantern. The light inside shifted from tones of blue and purple, looking purely magical as Aysel dug into a pocket of her bag for a coin purse. She took out two small, copper coins with the centers missing, and handed them over to the old man in exchange for the lantern which she carefully slipped into her bag.

"Send your grandmother my good wishes," he finally said, twisting the end of his beard.

"I will. Thank you," Aysel said, starting to walk away.

But the lantern seller touched her shoulder gently, "Wait. For your boots."

He came out from behind the stall, uncapping a small bottle of wine, and began sprinkling droplets over her boots. Aysel didn't argue over receiving the blessing, holding out each foot in turn for him to dribble the liquid on.

There were a lot of rituals she still didn't understand. But the old man had been a friend of her grandmother for decades, so Aysel knew there was nothing nefarious behind it.

When he was finished he gave her a sad smile, which pulled at all the good wrinkles on his face, "Good luck. Keep an eye on that watch of yours."

"I will, thanks again."

"Always willing to help out an old friend." With a tip of his hat he went back behind his makeshift counter.

Looking at her watch as she stepped away from his stall, Aysel bit her lip. Just over an hour and a half had passed. But that still left plenty of time for her other stops before the sun began to rise. Hurrying to the end of an alley, Aysel stopped in front of an old blue door with peeling paint. There was no knocker or bell, and a sign above the door was no longer readable. Luckily the lock could be opened with a simple skeleton key that she kept on a string around her neck. As the tumblers clicked into place, she glanced around to ensure no one was watching her. Even if someone did follow, it was unlikely they'd be able to get through the door. Sometimes something just wasn't for everyone.

Pulling a cord above her head to turn on the faint overhead light within the cramped space, Aysel waited until she heard the tumblers lock again. A rotary dial phone—just the circular plate with numbers one through zero listed counterclockwise—was mounted on the wall in front of her. She turned the dial to the nine three times and listened for the click of the tumblers before opening the door again.

The foggy street was nearly empty as Aysel exited the little phone box at her next stop. She was careful to stay on the flagstone immediately outside the phone box so she wouldn't have to begin counting her steps yet. Pulling her hood up over her head, she strained to see through the gloom. Street lamps flickered a sickening green and the air smelled faintly of petrichor. It might have looked like a picturesque little village, but it gave her the heebie jeebies. Even in the dead of night, the air was warm and muggy and sounds were muffled as someone moved through the mist. Her grandmother had always warned her not to stay long in this particular otherworld.

Aysel checked her watch, noting that it was just after ten. Shadows shifted along in step with her in the soupy fog as she began to hurry down the cobblestone road. She'd never seen anyone's face there, and she wanted to keep it that way. This dreary village was the only place to get proper candles.

She walked exactly a hundred paces, with the green light of the street lamps her only company before she turned left. By then the echoing had started. The dampened sound of her own footsteps repeating and bouncing off the stone walls of the buildings that stood just beyond the mist. Pulling her jacket tighter around her and making sure her hood was still masking her face, she counted out the next hundred paces then took another left.

This was usually when the singing began. It was important not to make any acknowledgment of it for fear of becoming entrapped by whatever was calling out into the summer evening. Aysel finished counting the final hundred paces and again took a left. Out of habit, she knew where the door handle was and reached forward into the muck, pulled it open, and quickly stepped inside.

A bell rang joyfully. It was much brighter inside the shop, filled with candles of every shape and size, flames of every color bending slightly from her entering the shop. Aysel pulled out a plain white mask that looked a bit like bone and put it on before she approached the counter and gently rang the silver bell that was sitting there. The clear tone struck at a memory Aysel wasn't even aware she still had. Rushing cool water and the sound of hooves lingered in the back of her mind.

She wasn't given much chance to wonder about the long-forgotten memory as the proprietor of the shop appeared from a back room. The cloaked figure wore a similarly plain mask, though it was black.

"What can I do for you, child?" the proprietor asked, their voice warm, like honey in a cup of tea.

"I was hoping to acquire some beeswax candles."

"Ah," the proprietor moved deliberately, going to a set of drawers, "And what color flame?"

"Purple, if you have it."

"Unusual choice."

"Purple is my grandmother's favorite color."

Nodding, the proprietor opened a drawer and pulled out two paper-wrapped, pillar candles. They paused for a moment and seemed to consider something, "Your grandmother must be a unique type of person."

"She's definitely special."

"She must be for you to have traveled here for some candles."

"It was on my way."

The proprietor tilted their head to the side, "Do you traverse between the worlds often?"

"I will be. Going forward."

"I see. Then you are unique as well."

"I don't know about that."

"Oh? Traveling betwixt otherworlds isn't unique?"

"Not to me, I guess," Aysel said with a shrug.

"No, I suppose it wouldn't be strange then." They set the candles down on the counter, "There is a matter of the price of course."

Aysel smiled behind her mask and went right over to a game board set up at the far end of the countertop. While it appeared that the game had already been started, some of the pieces were missing, with crude, folded paper tokens standing in their place. She took a small, black stone from her bag and placed it on the board where it shifted into one of the missing game pieces.

"You've been here before then?" the proprietor asked, coming around the counter to inspect the new game piece.

"I have."

They studied her for a long moment, "Hrm…was it your grandmother that taught you so well?"

She nodded, "My grandmother's been training me since I was little."

"To take her place?"

Aysel felt her breath hitch, "Yes."

"I accept your payment then, child," the proprietor said, holding out the candles to Aysel. "Would you care to play?"

It was tempting; her partner didn't know how to play. Yet. "I would, but it would keep my grandmother waiting."

The proprietor nodded, "Of course. We wouldn't want to delay you then. Perhaps another time."

They raised their hand, the door opening and the mist parting to reveal a courtyard with a well in the center.

Bowing her head, Aysel slipped the candles into her bag and waved as she left the establishment. She didn't waste any time crossing the courtyard to the well. Exactly one hundred paces from the doorway. Climbing up onto the stone lip of the well, the fog began to close back around her. A popping sound in the distance foreshadowed the appearance of a bobbing, blue light. Another popping sound formed a second glowing ember, hanging in the air. She clutched the key hanging around her neck and lined up the bow, the little loop at the end of the key, to her sight line. As she looked through the bow, she could see several cloaked, shadowy figures approaching, surrounded by the wisps.

A voice in the distance softly began singing,

> *'Petals drip down into the river,*
> *Escaping even the ferryman's quiver,*
> *Best be nimble, even quick.*
> *With a coin for the ferryman,*
> *Or a lamp for the merryman,*
> *Don't forget your candlestick.'*

A shiver ran down Aysel's spine as she froze. The ticking of her watch began echoing in her ears as the figures loomed closer and closer, surrounding her. As the shop bell rang again signaling that the door had shut, she shook herself. All around her, the mist and fog were rushing back into place, obscuring the figures and the wisps. Without bothering to look at her watch, Aysel jumped into the well, a warm breeze and the sound of wind whistling, greeting her as she plunged into the darkness.

Falling through the well left Aysel standing in a circle of stones by a crossroads as the wind howled by. Taking the mask off, Aysel retreated to the edge of the woods that butted up against the road on one side. She sucked in a deep breath, letting the tension escape from her body. At least she wouldn't have to go back there any time soon. Her watch had stopped just before midnight. A bit too close for her liking actually. Winding it again, it began to gently tick on.

While she waited, Aysel pulled out a sandwich wrapped in a cloth. As she unwrapped it, she found a marigold that had been lovingly slipped between the wrapping. Tucking it behind her ear, she started to eat, hoping that she wouldn't have to wait long. There was still one other stop after the crossroads.

The wind whipped through the trees which gave very little protection. She doubted she'd even be able to light a fire for warmth. Nonetheless, drawing the attention of the locals with a fire was never a good idea. No matter how unseasonably cold it was for midsummer.

Howling slowly gave way to the sound of hooves and barking, the pandemonium thundering in her ears. A chariot surrounded by hounds and a cloaked warband burst from the clouds and came to a calamitous halt in the middle of the crossroads. As the band stopped, it became clear that the horse pulling the chariot was beginning to go lame. The driver of the chariot threw down her reins and quickly went to check on the horse, gently rubbing its shoulder.

"Shhhhshh, it's alright," she said to it as it made sounds of pain.

Aysel got to her feet and cautiously approached the band, "I might be able to assist you, my lady."

White cloak rippling in the wind, the chariot driver turned towards Aysel, pulling her hood back to inspect Aysel more closely. She was at least a head taller than Aysel, and her cloak disguised her wide shoulders.

"Mortals should be wary of our band, lest they want to join us," she held out a delicate hand for Aysel to kiss.

Pressing her lips to the woman's knuckles, Aysel shivered as the air suddenly turned cold.

"You look familiar though. Have we met before?"

"No, my lady. Though some say I resemble my grandmother."

"Ah." Recognition dawned in her eyes. "That must be it," the woman said with a sad smile.

"Can I see if I might be able to help?" Aysel asked.

"If you can spare the time."

With a nod, Aysel approached the misty white horse, gently stroking its mane. The hounds watched her, but kept their distance. Carefully lifting the horse's front hoof and inspecting it, it looked like they'd walked through a patch of thorns and had snagged their leg, leaving a web of cuts. Taking the marigold from behind her ear, she crushed the flower, rubbing it between her palms until it was paste-like. Then she carefully rubbed the paste into the wounds and wrapped the leg with the cloth from her dinner.

The horse nuzzled her shoulder, its black eyes reminding her of how the river looked at night.

"You seem to have a way with her. Have you been around horses before?"

Aysel nodded before stepping away from the horse, "Yes, in a way."

"Perhaps you could join us? We're always in search of new members."

"I have to get back to my grandmother," Aysel said, though the prospect was enticing.

"Then take this as your reward," the

woman said, pulling a broken bowstring from the purse at her waist.

Gently closing her hand around the sinew, Aysel bowed her head as the woman got back into her chariot. As she picked up the reins, she pulled her hood back up, and the hounds started to become restless, "If only every mortal I met at a crossroads could be as kind as you. Take care, young one. Give your grandmother my love. She is lucky to have you."

"I will, thank you."

The woman flicked the reins and her horse leaped forward, hooves climbing into the air. As the rest of the band followed, the thundering sound began to fade, leaving the faintest whisper on the wind as they continued their hunt into the night. Aysel returned to the tree line, picking up her bag and eating the last few bites of her sandwich as she walked through the towering trees, comforted by the quiet swish of the branches overhead.

The trees became denser, nearly impassable, before giving way to a field of tall grass and wildflowers. As the grasses moved together they sang a hushed, yet familiar song to the tune of the bubbling river that was somewhere out of sight. While she walked, Aysel knew that time was passing, but it was impossible to gauge by just looking at her surroundings, and the hands-on her watch spun forward and backward. The soft grass sprang back into place behind her, obscuring the path as she went. This was the hardest test by far, trusting that there was an end to the wall of stalks. But she could feel something tugging her forward, taking her to where she needed to go.

Her watch's ticking was barely audible over the sounds of the grasses brushing against each other, but Aysel knew that it had slowed as she emerged onto the bank of the river. Anchored in the center of the river was a long, flat bottomed boat with a single passenger hunched at the tiller. The water was perfectly still, like a plane of dark glass, and didn't reflect the sea of stars that hung above them.

"Come, child, there's no going back the way you came," the figure called from across the water, beckoning her forward.

Ensuring her hood was still in place, Aysel set one foot on the surface of the river, the water rising to cup her foot, then the other. She inched cautiously across the dark ribbon that cut through the field. A part of her had worried that she'd fall, but it was like walking through sand, solid, yet still flowing.

When she reached the boat, the figure offered her a hand and helped her in. Between them sat a small table with a map carved into it. A tiny version of the boat moved along the river that spanned the center of the map. Several clay jugs of wine and oil were wrapped in protective cloth and leaned against the sides of the boat.

Aysel peered at the figure through the darkness, unsure of what to expect. Her grandmother had never told her much about this part. The figure's eyes reflected the glow of starlight.

"It seems someone gave you some protection from the river," the figure stated, pointing a withered hand at Aysel's boots. Tiny beads of light covered them where the lantern seller had dripped the rice wine. She'd have to remember to thank him for that.

"I guess so."

The ferrier deliberately moved back to their place at the tiller. An easy silence hung between them, almost like the figure was waiting for Aysel to continue.

"I'm sorry, I'm not really sure what I need to do here."

"Most don't when they get here. Your grandmother followed the boat along the riverbank until nearly sunrise."

Biting her lip, Aysel scanned the pristine bank of the river, "Is that bad?"

The figure didn't respond. Probably because they felt it was a silly question. Spending any amount of time in a foreign otherworld, even in Aysel's new profession was incredibly dangerous. Those that traveled between them regularly carried protections, charms, or spells to keep them from harm. Unless their position itself granted a measure of protection.

"Do you have something to offer me, young one?"

There was only one correct answer, yet so many forms in which she could. And there was no way to take it back once it was done. Taking her hood, she pulled it back, revealing her long hair, plaited and pinned to the back of her head in a coil.

While she couldn't see the figure's facial features, she had the distinct feeling they were smiling, "It's always good to formally meet a colleague. Past or future. Are you ready?"

Aysel nodded and watched as the figure dipped two of their fingers, first into one of the jugs of oil, then into the wine, before leaning over the map. She closed her eyes and the figure smeared the mixture across them. It was warm, and the wine stung when it seeped in under her eyelids. But when she opened them again, her vision was cloudy, as if she was trying to look through a thick mist.

"Now, take this, and give her my farewells," the figure said, pressing one of the small jugs of wine into her hands. "You should know the way now."

Wrapping her arms around the jug, Aysel tried to blink the mist from her eyes. It was persistent though, and she knew her time was up as the ticking sound from her watch grew louder in her ears. After managing to slip the jug of wine into her bag, she stood up and took a deep breath before stepping over the edge into the river.

The cool water embraced Aysel, carrying her to her final destination as the sky began to lighten. It dripped from her hair as she crawled through the mud to the bank, but the spirits the river carried paid her little mind. Her vision cleared once she pulled herself up alongside an old, wooden dock. All around her lingered the dead, from the smallest animals to the poor souls of humans who had never been guided to their final rest. The warm summer air and the gentle hum of insects helped disguise the unusualness of the location.

Her grandmother helped her up onto the dock, a fuzzy blanket enveloping her, and wiped water from her face as she'd done many times before. Aysel didn't stop her, instead committing the moment to memory.

"You're late," her grandmother complained, finally content with how the wisps of fringe around Aysel's temples were laying.

Glancing at her watch, Aysel saw the hour hand nearing four.

"And don't blame your grandfather's watch. It runs perfectly for being as old as it is."

"I know, grandmother. I just had to fetch a few things."

Shaking her head in annoyance, her grandmother said, "There's no use in making such a fuss about this. It's completely natural."

"I wanted to. And your friends send their

good wishes."

The old woman chuckled, "Oh those old grumps. They can visit anytime they like. It's one of the few perks of this work."

Aysel set down her bag and began pulling out everything she'd collected: the lantern, the candles, and finally the jug of wine. When her grandmother saw the jug of wine her expression softened. Aysel kept the bowstring twisted in her pocket for now.

"You should have let me bring you."

"I'll have to do it on my own from now on, so I figured this was a good time to start."

"Well, let's get this in the boat then. It's about time I showed you how to find the right current."

Nodding, Aysel left her bag, boots, and sweatshirt on the dock while her grandmother moved the other items to the tiny boat anchored there. It bobbed in the water as she stepped into it, but this little boat was practically a second home. Her grandmother had already set the candles up in the places on either side of the seat in the front, lit them, and hung the lantern off the prow. She had produced two tiny stoneware cups and was pouring them each some wine as Aysel gently pushed them away from the dock and sat down at the tiller as the water at the front of the boat rippled.

"Now, remember Current and Tide are going to want to veer you to the left bank, keep them centered until we get to the first gate."

That gave Aysel cause to smile as two scaly heads slipped above the waterline for a moment, "Still causing trouble, are they?"

"Always. Feisty devils," her grandmother said warmly, dipping her hand into the water to stroke the long snouts of the kelpies harnessed to the boat. "Let's go now, loves."

"Will they open for me? The gates?"

"Of course they will. You're more than ready, dear. You have to be confident. There's no reason to fear," her grandmother said, settling in and sipping at her wine.

Clasping her hand around the tiller, Aysel watched the dark water carefully, making tiny adjustments as the kelpie tried to wander off course. They drifted in silence until the first gate, guarded by two statues so old and worn it was impossible to tell who they might have been in the past. Aysel stood, holding her hands out in front of her for a long moment before willing the ancient doors to part.

She felt the old lock in her mind and

willed the internal mechanisms to turn. The weathered hinges groaned, sending waves of displaced darkness cascading towards the banks as the doors began to open. It didn't take nearly as much effort compared to the times she'd opened them under her grandmother's guidance.

They creaked and the boat jerked forward as they passed through it.

"Your parents would be proud of you. And Moira must be," her grandmother said quietly as the gate closed behind them.

"I know," Aysel kept hold of the long arm of the tiller as she stood.

Raising an eyebrow, her grandmother continued, "Is she worried? I know all this is strange to people outside the family."

"A little bit. But I think she understands it now."

"That's good. I knew I always liked her, for some reason."

Aysel smiled a bit.

"There we go, you should be celebrating. This is an important day for you."

"I know, it's just hard."

"Careful here, there's a little dip just before the next gate," her grandmother warned.

"Does it get easier?"

"Once you know the river it does."

She shook her head, "No, I mean, taking people down the river." The second set of doors parted without issue, "With people you know."

Her grandmother gave her a sad smile, "I can't tell you if it gets easier. Some days go by and you can't keep from crying. Others you can. Goodbyes are always difficult. Whether it's a day or an eternity."

Aysel didn't say anything more as they went through the third, then fourth, fifth and sixth gates. With each gate passed, she could feel the flow growing stronger, and Current and Tide tugging harder at the little boat. As the final gate loomed in the gray misty water before them, Aysel didn't make any moves to open it. She sat down and looked across the boat at her grandmother.

"Dear, you can't delay this. It's my time."

Taking the bowstring from her pocket, Aysel leaned forward and wrapped one end around her grandmother's wrist.

"Aysel?" her grandmother asked gently.

She blinked back tears as she wrapped the other end around her wrist and the sinew turned into a red cord that broke into two, "This way you won't really be gone. We'll be connected."

Her grandmother pulled her into a

tight hug, "I've lived a full, wonderful life. Just remember, this isn't goodbye. Tonight might end, but the sun rises again and again. One day you'll come down the river to see me again. Until then, you have all your memories of me."

"Memories aren't the same."

Kissing her forehead, her grandmother removed her dark cloak and wrapped it around Aysel's shoulders. Even though it looked heavy, it barely weighed anything, "You're ready for this. I know you are. You're my granddaughter."

Aysel used the edge of the cloak to wipe away her tears, keeping hold of her grandmother's hand as she stood again, staring at the final gate. The red cord wrapped around her wrist felt tight.

"I bid you luck on your journey beyond," Aysel said, her voice trembling as she let go of her grandmother's hand to part the final gates. The boat didn't continue to flow down the river this time; instead, the dark water lit up with a bright silvery glow. Her grandmother took the lantern from the hook on the prow and gave her a final smile before stepping out of the boat.

And just as suddenly as if she'd stepped through another portal, Aysel's grandmother was gone, and the final gates closed again.

Her grandmother's hand was cold in hers when Aysel came back to the world of the living. Tears had dripped down her cheeks, and she could sense Moira hovering, waiting for the right time to say something. Laying her grandmother's hand down across her still chest, Aysel spotted the nearly invisible red thread that connected them both when it caught the light.

Moira rested a hand on her shoulder, "Aysel?"

She got up and wrapped her arms around Moira, burying her face in her partner's shoulder. Moira ran her fingers through Aysel's hair then up and down her back gently.

"She lived a long happy life."

Aysel nodded, sniffling, then pulled back, resting her hands on the bump between them, "I was just hoping…"

"I know she'll keep an eye on them," Moira said, looking down at her protruding belly, "Are you going to be okay?"

"Yes," Aysel said.

"How were her friends? Should I have sent something with you for them?"

"No, it's okay. Can't get them used to gifts."

"But muffins or cookies would be fine, right?"

"I'm not sharing your cooking with them unless you want a bunch of reapers showing up for dinner."

Moira looked horrified for a moment, "Would they just…show up?"

Aysel laughed, "Probably not. But it's best not to tempt the fates."

"No, of course not. At least not until the baby is born. Do they eat regular food?"

"We're not inviting them for dinner," Aysel said firmly, kissing Moira. She glanced out the window in time to catch a white cat slipping from the windowsill. The bell on its collar rang brightly as the red cord around her wrist tugged gently, and she knew that Moira was right.

Death was just a part of living. The important part was how you spent your time.

STAR
CHASER

STAR CHASER

GREYSEN & EDWIN(A)

THE BUZZ OF INSECTS filled the background of the sticky air. Blades of grass swayed in and out of sight. Slowly, the stars twinkled into view as the sky darkened and revealed the dusty galaxies above.

The crackle of a voice over the ham radio nestled in the blanket nearby said, "Ursa Major online and heading out for retrieval for the night. Over."

"This is Control, copy that Ursa Major. Star fall is scheduled to start at 21:17. Over."

"Fantastic. It's gonna be a great night.

Ursa Major out."

A single streak of light kicked off the evening's starfall, cutting across the sky in an arc. It burned brighter the closer it got to the ground, finally casting a flash of multicolored sparks as the star crashed down. Sitting up, little Edwin grabbed their binoculars to scan the area. A cloud of dust zipping towards the site, made them grin widely.

"Edwin honey, it's time to come in!" their mother called from the house down the other side of the hill.

They wanted to see the star chaser collect the first star of the night, but the shadow of their mother in the doorway would linger until they came home. Giving the eruption of sparks one last glance, Edwin scooped up the radio and ran down the hill.

"You know it's past your bedtime Edwin," their mother scolded, catching them in a hug at the kitchen door.

"But the sky is clear enough to see the start of the star fall!"

"And yet, you still have school tomorrow."

"I know," Edwin admitted sheepishly.

"Off to bed with you," their mother said, steering them inside.

Edwin took the creaking stairs two at a time, kicking off their shoes before climbing into the window seat that looked over the meadow. They picked up a rock with swirling veins of silver that sat proudly on their window sill and clutched it to their chest.

"One day, that's gonna be me," they whispered, their eyes locked on the brilliant streaks of light as they crossed the early evening sky.

Dusk brought swift relief from the desert heat as the sun dipped below the horizon. The earliest rising stars blinked away sleep, twinkling in the distance. Greysen was finishing up her coffee, watching the sky turn from blue to pink and orange before taking on hues of purple from the balcony of the watchtower.

There was a loud ding from inside, the volume increasing as Cilla opened the door, "Today's roster just started coming through."

Greysen held up her coffee cup as an explanation, "I'm almost done."

Cilla leaned against the railing next to

her, "That sunset is pretty."

Greysen hummed in agreement as she closed her eyes, enjoying the breeze wafting through her cropped hair. Lips pressed against her temple, and Cilla's warm breath sent shivers through her.

"You can finish your coffee on the road."

"Alright, alright," Greysen sighed, stealing another kiss before Cilla herded her inside.

A pen was scratching away in her notebook, detailing the evening's pickup coordinates. She glanced down at its progress, noting that it was going to be a busy night.

"Did someone call in?"

"It looks like it. Some of those coordinates look like they're on Marie's route."

"Huh, I'll have to send her a message."

The pen fell over, nearly rolling off the desk after it finished the final entry for the day. Greysen made a quick count of the stops as she began entering the locations into her hand-held nav-system.

"Seventeen," Greysen said mostly to herself with a click of her tongue.

"Then you better get a move on if you want to finish before sun up," Cilla said, ignoring Greysen's gloomy look.

"They gave me one of Marie's."

"Don't start any fights," Cilla held out Greysen's bag and leather jacket.

"But it's seventeen pickups," Greysen whined, recounting the list for a fifth time.

"There are no unlucky numbers."

"Maybe for you."

"Go before you make yourself later."

"Alright, alright, I'm going!" Greysen groaned, "Give Eleanor a kiss for me."

"Love you, hopefully it won't keep you out too late," Cilla replied, kissing her goodbye as she slipped a wrapped sandwich and a paper bag of cookies into Greysen's pack. "Eleanor's big recital is tomorrow. Don't drive like a maniac."

"Love you too. And my driving is just fine."

"Shoo!"

Cilla hurried Greysen back out to the balcony where Greysen's hoverbike was parked. She pulled on her jacket and attached her bag to the rack, checking a few components as she went. Her nav-system attached to the steering column and booted up the crystal on-board computer. A cluster of dots appeared on the mapping system, indicating the evening's pickups, and the computer plotted the most efficient route.

The hover bike purred to life as she inserted the crystal key and turned on the engine. She pulled on her helmet as she straddled the bike. Static obscured the visor for a moment as the helmet synced with the nav-system and hoverbike's computer. With all the system checks clear, she revved the bike and opened the throttle.

Shooting off the watchtower's platform, the hoverbike quickly adjusted to the terrain height, giving the bike a downward arch until it landed just inches above the ground. She sped off towards the fading sunlight, the outlines of the chimney-shaped rock formations in the distance.

It was quiet out on the wild expanse of desert, save for the hum of her hoverbike and the soft alerts from the nav-system. Sagebrush and juniper trees whipped by, and blended into the wash of white and purple blooms of the desert flowers as they closed their petals for the night.

"This is control, do you read, Auriga?" a gruff voice asked in her ear.

"Yup, on my way out to the first pickup of the night," she replied in a clipped tone.

"Looks like you're running late."

Greysen muted her radio so she wouldn't say something untoward on a public frequency. "Just by a minute. I'll more than make up the time."

"Reckless driving is inadvisable."

Thanks, mom, Greysen thought. "I'm always safe. Do you need anything else from me? I nearly have a visual." There was a bright flash above her followed by a streak of green and blue plasma crossing the sky.

"Did you receive your updated roster for the evening?"

"I did."

"Then that's all."

"Copy that, Control. Auriga out," she said, decisively tapping her comm off and racing in the direction of her first pickup.

Another flash of light erupted as the star Greysen was chasing crashed into the ground ahead of her. She shielded her eyes and slowed down as the shock wave from the impact rolled past her and off into the desert. Stopping a few yards from the edge of the smoldering crater the star had created, she shut off her hover-bike.

The star was sputtering blue and green flames as it cooled rapidly. Greysen pulled a round, glass bottle from a compartment on her bike and tossed it into the crater. When the bottle broke, the contents quickly expanded to encompass the crater in a cooling solution. Beads of sweat rolled down Greysen's temples, dripping onto her jacket and drying almost instantly in residual heat. There would be hell to pay if she returned home with burns on her hands again, so Greysen pulled a pair of heavy gloves from her back pocket.

Grabbing a containment cylinder from the back of her hover-bike, Greysen slid down the side of the crater. Heat was still rolling off the glowing lump at the center, but it had cooled enough that the rubber wasn't melting from the soles of her shoes. A few sparks flew off, tinkling like tiny bells just before they faded into the darkness. She knelt next to the fallen star and gingerly picked up the swirling ball of light.

Closing her eyes, she let the warmth and light wash over her, washing away her surroundings as the star gave her a glimpse at the wish it was carrying.

A lush garden filled her mind's eye, overgrown with wildflowers, but with purpose. Bees buzzed lazily from flower to flower and in the distance, Greysen could see a couple laughing together as they picked strawberries.

As quickly as the vision had come, it was gone again, leaving Greysen alone in the dark desert. The feeling of being inside someone else's dream was strange, like trying to make a jacket fit that had been tailored to someone else's body. It was uncomfortable enough to remember that it belonged to a stranger. She smiled as she sealed the star into the cylinder, the delivery address appearing in bold text as soon as it was closed.

One down, sixteen to go...

With the first pickup of the night completed, Greysen placed the cylinder safely into the compartment on her bike and pulled up the next location marker on her route.

There was little rhyme or reason to where stars fell in relation to the wisher or dreamer. Greysen had always thought that the stars ended up close to a chaser that would appreciate them. Or had the countenance to handle its contents, as not all dreams were happy. It was a treat to pickup up a wish that drew out a smile.

After making it through a few more pickups, Greysen's communicator buzzed to life again, "Auriga, this is Pyxis."

"Good to hear you, *Markeb*. What's up?"

"Just curious if you wanted to meet up for dinner? My nav puts us crossing paths on our next pickup."

"Yeah, I'm up for that."

"I'll see you soon then."

She selected the intersection of their

routes and added the stop. When Greysen arrived, Marie was already waiting, crouched next to a little fire, sipping from her thermos. The older woman waved as Greysen parked and grabbed the dinner that Cilla had packed for her.

"Did your lovely wife pack you any of those wonderful cookies of hers?"

With a smile, Greysen pulled out a bag of cookies with Marie's name scrawled on it and tossed them to her, "Of course."

The older woman caught the package with her free hand and set them safely on her lap, "She spoils us."

"She does."

"And how's the kiddo?"

"Always coming up with new and surprising ways to be herself."

Marie grinned, "I remember those days. You'll miss them once she's a teenager with all those emotions bouncing around."

"I think I'll wish for her to stay little and cute forever."

"And trap all that deviousness into such a tiny package?" Marie asked with a knowing twinkle in her eye.

"You're just determined to constantly make me question being a parent."

"Always. Have any interesting pickups yet?" Marie asked.

Greysen shrugged, "Just the usual. Kids dreaming about pet dragons to torment their siblings. Adults wanting life to be simpler."

"You do tend to get all the best pet dreams."

"If Cilla wasn't allergic, we'd have a menagerie."

"I'm sure there's a spell worker that could help with the allergies," Marie said, her eyes sparkling in the firelight. "My brother's drake has some hatchlings on the way."

"Now you're just trying to get me in trouble."

"Never dear. You know some star catchers used to ride dragons or griffins before bikes became more popular."

"Cilla would definitely kill me if I tried to ride a dragon or a griffin for work. She hates hover-bikes as it is."

"They're perfectly safe."

"Try convincing her of that."

"Well, better to have an overprotective wife I suppose," Marie mused. "Oh, I had a pickup a few weeks ago that I thought you might find interesting."

Greysen watched curiously as Marie pulled herself up and hopped over to her bike on her lone leg, digging around in her saddlebags until she produced a cylinder. Standard procedure stated that stars should be dropped off at a distribution and shipping center the morning after collection. Holding onto one was tantamount to mail theft. When Marie held out the cylinder in question, Greysen noticed that the label looked like the spine of a book fading when left on a windowsill and where it would usually have a delivery address, was blank.

"Did the address fade?"

"Nope, never appeared. I've seen it happen a few times."

"Do you know why there's no address?"

"I figure there's something wrong with the magic identifying the owner. Just like people, magic isn't perfect."

"What happens to them if an address never appears?"

"Most of the time, they sit collecting dust at a distro-center."

"And there's no way of figuring out who they belong to?"

"If someone knows what they're doing, they might be able to. But I got into this work because I'm not that talented with magic, so I wouldn't have a clue where to start."

Greysen slid her nail along the thick glass, tilting the star back and forth so it would reignite some of its natural glow. The gray stone threw off some multicolored sparks, but it was far dimmer than a fresh star.

"That's heartbreaking. Everyone should be united with their wishes and dreams."

"Why don't you hang onto that one then?"

"Are you sure?"

Marie nodded, "Maybe that clever brain of yours will figure something out?"

A wet nose pressed against the back of her leg. The furry stranger looked up, brown eyes dull as they longingly gazed at the sandwich just out of reach. His scruffy, wiry haired golden fur was dull, and he had been limping along behind her on the seemingly endless walk from the corner shop back home. There was no one else around, and the dog didn't have a collar around its neck.

Kneeling, she pulled some of the turkey out of

her sandwich and held it out for the dog. His tongue swiped over a scraggly beard and whiskers before he gobbled up the cold cuts, tail starting to wag.

"Well, aren't you a cutie? Where's your home?"

The dog sniffed the air, hinting that it was still hungry.

"I always wanted a dog, but I just have too much going on with my nephew coming to live with me. You must belong to someone..."

Licking her hand, the dog turned those big brown eyes on her again.

She sighed, "I guess I could take you home, and we could find out who you belong to? And until then, my nephew can help take care of you. Would you like that, old man?"

The dog nuzzled into her. It would be nice to have another body in the house. Maybe her nephew would come out of his shell a little bit with the help their new friend?

Edwin pocketed the long faded lump of stardust that they had had since before they could remember. The star had belonged to their mother and had been one of her most precious possessions that they had begged her to let them hold onto. Now that she was gone, they carried it everywhere.

'*A dream of a loved one is better than any picture,*' she used to tell them.

But what use was a dream when that person was gone?

Peeking into their classroom, Edwin wished that the school would let them bring dogs to class. Polaris wouldn't bother anyone. He was old and just wanted to be near people and sleep most of the day.

"Edwin?" their teacher's voice called, "Class is about to start."

Shuffling into the room, Edwin went to their desk, setting the old star in its place in the corner.

No one really wanted to be in summer school. Running amok with friends during the heat of the day, sticky popsicles dripping all over was much more preferred to being stuck indoors. But Edwin had resigned themselves to a summer of extra homework to catch up to their classmates. It wasn't as if they had friends to roam the desert with anyhow. Just Polaris.

The chatter of their fellow students died

down as the teacher stood up in front of the blackboard. Her smile matched her cheery dress covered in brightly colored math equations.

"I'd like everyone to take out the letters we've been working on so we can get those finished up."

Lifting the top of their desk up, Edwin fished around for their letter. It wasn't going to be sent to anyone. It was just supposed to be practice. Like having an imaginary pen pal. But Edwin had figured if they had to write to someone imaginary, they might as well write to someone who was dead.

A thud turned all the students' attention as Edwin's star toppled off the edge of their desk and onto the floor.

Edwin's neighbor looked down at the gray lump by their feet and kicked it back toward Edwin.

"Don't kick it!" a classmate exclaimed.

"Well I don't want to touch it- who knows what Eddie dreams about!"

The teacher tried to offer Edwin a reassuring smile as she picked up the star with a tissue, "Why don't we keep this at home from now on, okay Edwin?"

Edwin was good at not crying anymore.

It had been a year since their parents had died and he had to move to the bleak desert town with their aunt. Gingerly slipping the star back into their pocket, Edwin stared at the letter on their desk.

Dear Mom,

why did you and Dad have to leave me? I thought I was your wish...

The remaining hours of class ticked by in a painful lull. Focusing on regular school was hard enough but extra school was even worse. When the bell rang, signaling the end of the day, Edwin gathered up their backpack and started to file out with the rest of the kids hoping to salvage some of the remaining sunshine.

"Edwin, can we talk for a bit?"

Plonking down their bag, Edwin tried to ignore the curious glances from their remaining classmates. It wasn't as if Edwin had anywhere else to be. Besides taking Polaris for a walk. Or staring up at the sky waiting for the stars to show for the night.

"Yeah?"

The teacher shuffled around some papers

on her desk before pulling out Edwin's letter and straightening it. "I was hoping we could talk about the letter that you wrote…"

Edwin tried not to roll their eyes. One of the therapists Aunt Narine had brought them to had wanted to talk at length about how they were dealing with their parents' deaths. And the anger that Edwin seemed to be harboring. This teacher didn't seem much different. She was trying to be kind and understanding, but really she just wanted Edwin to admit that they were sad and angry at the circumstances and then to move on like it had never happened.

"Did I do it wrong?" Edwin asked a little defensively.

"No, no…I just wondered why you wrote it to your mother?"

"You said it could be to anyone."

"Well yes…"

"I'll do it over if that's what you want."

"No, Edwin. I just wanted to know why you wanted to write to your mother?"

"If we weren't going to send the letters, then no one was going to answer anyhow."

She pressed her lips together tightly before saying, "You're right. I'll see you tomorrow Edwin."

Grabbing their bag, Edwin was glad that their hot tears waited until they were outside the school building to start flowing.

Greysen's shelf of address-less stars had quickly overgrown its initial space and soon taken over the windowsills around the watchtower. Cilla had tried to temper the collection in the beginning, but within a month had given in and relocated some of the house plants so the stars could have more space. Any time a destination-less star came into the local distribution center, the manager set it aside for Greysen to come and pick it up. In his opinion, they were better off collecting dust somewhere else.

First, she'd tried testing the labels themselves to see if they were the faulty piece in the equation. But the carefully removed scraps of the labels worked perfectly on other containment cylinders. Greysen had even been able to patch together fully sized labels from those little fragments. Transferring the stars into new cylinders hadn't solved the problem either. And while stars could store for a long time without losing their magic, Greysen was concerned about their longevity.

"Find anything useful?" Cilla asked, watering one of her plants while Eleanor was marking her way through another coloring book and Greysen flipped through an old research text on the nature of wish and dream stars.

"No," Greysen rubbed her temples. It was probably the driest text she'd read since college.

Leaning over Greysen's shoulder, "'*Containment cylinders must be magically reinforced to withstand extreme temperatures and pressure...*' well obviously! When is that book even from?"

"Before our grandparents were born?" Greysen offered.

"That's ancient, mumma," Eleanor commented from her coloring perch at the table.

"It is," Greysen agreed.

Cilla asked, "Maybe you need to try looking somewhere else?"

"I feel like I've read all the research on stars that's out there."

"I mean, stop trying to find the answer books and start looking in the stars."

"Ha ha, very funny."

"I'm serious," Cilla balanced her watering can on her hip. "Have you gone through all the wishes and dreams to find any trends in why they might not have addresses?"

"Well, no." While peeking at the wishes contained in the stars that the chasers collected was an accepted part of the job, it was more taboo to do so with stars others had picked up.

"Then maybe it's time to try a new avenue of investigation. Because I'd like to tame the influx of your collection."

"But the stardust is pretty, mummy. If they all get sent away then the tower won't sparkle every night!" Eleanor protested.

Picking up Eleanor, Cilla spun her around, all her fluffy skirts splaying out. "True, but you don't have to sweep up all that dust. Unless you'd like to be in charge of it, Ellie-bug?"

Squealing with giggles, Eleanor shook her head, "No!"

"Then mumma needs to find their homes. Besides, you don't want to keep them from the people they belong to. That would be really sad."

Greysen looked over the rows of cylinders lined up around the watchtower.

"It's easier to view them in the dark."

"Just make sure you put down a towel or something so star dust doesn't get all over the table," Cilla said, leaning over to let Eleanor kiss

Greysen goodnight. "Let's go up and get ready for bed Ellie-bug."

"Sleep tight, Ellie," Greysen said before starting to clear a space on the table with a sigh.

The sun had been sinking in the sky for a while now, with the light fading into twilight. Greysen knew which star she wanted to start with, plucking the round containment unit from its spot on the windowsill. Dust rubbed off on her fingers before she set it down on the table and stared at it for a long moment.

She marked the container with a blue star next to the date, so she wouldn't try to record the same one twice. A date from almost a decade ago had been scribbled onto the cap with a marker along with a set of coordinates. Greysen presumed they related to when and where the star had been collected. She opened the cap which hissed as oxygen was allowed into the compartment for the first time in years and allowed the lump of dark gray rock tumble out into her palm.

A heart had been traced into the condensation on a window as trees and houses whipped past. The train car swayed gently, rumbling as it crossed streets, a distant sound of the crossing bells ringing penetrating the hum of music coming through headphones.

Sinking back into the seat, she mentally went through her to-do list. Homework for programming class. Trekking to the laundromat. Begging her roomie for advice on what to wear for her class presentation next week. Dark strands of hair fell into her eyes before quickly being pushed behind an ear. There were just a few stops left, then she'd be able to get off and hurry home before the rain started. Her mary janes were cute, but not really ideal for puddle dodging.

The train ground to a halt and other passengers filed past as they boarded.

She put a hand on top of her canvas bag of groceries, hoping that no one wanted to sit down next to her.

A boy about her age, curly hair drooping into his eyes, stopped next to her as the train began to move again, the carriage jerking and he dropped his phone on the seat next to her. Without thinking, she moved to pick it up and looked up at him as she held it out to him.

He smiled, "Thanks."

She found herself smiling goofily. He was kinda cute under all those curls.

"I like your headphones."

"What?" Oh stars, she sounded like an idiot!

He pointed to his head, "Your cat ear headphones. They're cute."

Was she blushing?

"Oh!" she cleared her throat and looked down at her lap. He was going to think she was weird.

The boy had sat down across the aisle and started flipping through his phone. The silence was definitely weird. But she caught him glancing back at her every so often.

Her stop arrived and she nearly jumped to her feet as it was announced overhead. Hauling her grocery bag over one shoulder, she headed to the door. As she stepped off the train, she caught the boy's eyes again and smiled to herself.

The vision ended abruptly, leaving Greysen feeling the budding hope from the dream. It was such a normal thing to dream about. Maybe the man was a crush? But there had been no familiarity.

Greysen grabbed a notebook and began hurriedly scribbling down everything from the smell of the man's cologne to what the houses the train passed had looked like. It wasn't a lot to go on. No names had been exchanged. But the train stops had been announced. Maybe someone would know who this star belonged to.

The sky was clear, the beach was full of seagulls scavenging for scraps, and the blue-green water was crashing gently along the sand. She was more than ready to try out her new swimming apparatus. With her single leg strapped into the prosthetic tail, she glanced back at her grandbabies, "What are we waiting for? Onward!"

With a bubble of giggles from them, they began pushing her modified wheelchair down to the surf. They wheeled her into the waves, all the way up to her waist.

"Is here okay, Grammie?"

"It's perfect lovies. Now let's hope Grammie remembers how to do this," she said, lifting herself out of the chair and into the incoming waves. The water caressed her as she got her bearings, floating on her back and testing out the long tail, its shining scales shimmered in the clear water. Tugging on her scuba mask, she dipped below the surface and was met with a kaleidoscope of underwater wildlife.

Schools of fish passed by on every side, darting around coral formations. Snorkeling with the prosthetic wasn't exactly like she'd swam before. But it was easy enough to adjust to. Out of the corners of her eyes, she spotted her grandchildren swimming along behind a family of sea turtles. The sun warmed *ocean had been the perfect way to enjoy their dream holiday.*

Edwin's teacher and Aunt Narine had started trading hushed phone calls about them on a weekly basis. None of Edwin's teachers had called home when their parents were still alive. All the therapists had said that their 'acting out' was natural. But Edwin wasn't acting out. At least they weren't trying to. They were on the phone together when Edwin came into the kitchen, Polaris following dutifully behind.

Narine quickly said her goodbyes and hung up, leaving a disquieting silence between them. She was doing her best not to mother them, but that made it all the more awkward between them.

"How was summer school today?" Narine asked as she went to the sink to begin washing the dishes.

"Fine."

"Did you make any friends?"

Edwin's answer hadn't changed since summer school had started, "The other kids already have friends."

Forcing a smile, Narine said, "Well, once regular school is back in session, there will be more kids to make friends with."

"I have some math homework to finish up," Edwin said, digging a notebook out of their backpack to take upstairs with them.

"Edwin…"

They stopped partway up one of the steps and turned back to Narine, "I'll be back down for dinner."

"Your teacher thought you might like to write another letter?"

"But I already redid the first one."

"Well, we've been chatting, and she has a friend who is married to one of the star chasers in town and I know you used to like watching the star falls. So, we thought you might want to write a letter to her?"

Polaris nudged the back of Edwin's knee, "Why? She wouldn't answer."

"We don't know that."

"I'll think about it," Edwin said and clamored up the stairs.

A real star chaser wouldn't have time to write back. They were always busy, chasing stars. Obviously. Writing back to some kid wasn't going to be high on their list of non-work things to do. Probably. But as Edwin sat down at their desk, they pulled out a blank sheet of paper and started writing.

Dear Mrs Star Chaser,

My aunt and teacher both said I should write to you. I wanted to be a star chaser when I was littler. Do you know why some people get certain stars? My mom kept one of hers for a long time and then gave it to me before she and my dad died. It's really faded now. But I can remember what the wish was still.

You don't have to write back. I know you're probably really busy with chasing all the stars.

- Edwin

Hi Edwin!

I was really excited to get your letter. I'm so glad that you wrote to me. I may be busy with work, but I can always make time for a letter or two. It's great that you wanted to be a star chaser. Is there something new you want to do when you grow up? (Don't worry, you've got plenty of time to decide!) We don't really know why some people get wishes or dreams via stars, but not others. There are some theories, like the wishes that come to you from the stars are what you wished for most, or are what magic knows is the best for you. But those are just theories. There are lots of things about stars we still don't know. Like why they can fall so far away from the person they belong to. Or why some stars don't have an address so we can't find the person they belong to. . I've been taking those home.

You're really lucky that your mom trusted you with her star. They're really precious things. You should definitely keep it safe.

- Greysen, your friendly neighborhood star chaser.

PS, you might know my daughter Eleanor. She's taking summer classes too.

Greysen yawned as she strode into the distribution center with a bag full of the night's batch of stars. The manager, an eternally grumpy man named Warren, was at the counter, skimming through a list while absently eating a sandwich. The center was usually a ghost town so early in the morning, but sitting on one of the worn, wooden benches was a little boy swinging his legs back and forth. A graying golden retriever was dutifully curled up under the bench.

"Put 'em in the back," Warren said between bites.

"Got anything new for me?"

"They're in the usual place."

Conversations with Warren were never very stimulating. Then again, she wasn't a very engaging human before coffee had settled in either.

Slipping into the sorting room, Greysen carefully emptied her bag of star cylinders onto the sorting table. It was still too early for the sorting team to be in, but Greysen tried to arrange her haul neatly for them. Once every cylinder was lined up, Greysen wandered farther back into the facility, past the neatly stacked boxes of empty containers, to a dusty corner where the addressless ones were left.

There were two containers in the bin that the distribution center had set aside for her. One appeared to be fairly new and had a note taped on it. The other had been retrieved decades ago and left to collect dust. A date had been scribbled on the label, but otherwise, it was blank like so many of the others.

Greysen restocked her bag with empty star containers and the two homeless stars before returning to the lobby. The kid was still sitting there with his dog, as if he'd been waiting for her.

"Excuse me?" he asked.

Greysen glanced at the manger who was engrossed in reading something on his tablet. "Yes?"

"Are you the one that's been taking all the addressless stars home?"

"Yeah, that's me. What can I do for you?"

"I'm Edwin. You responded to my letter."

She grinned at the slim boy, "Of course!

It's good to meet you, Edwin. What can I do for you?"

"I thought you might want some help."

Holding up her hand above Edwin's head she replied, "I think you might need to be a little taller before they let you on a hover-bike."

Edwin gave her a confused look.

"As much as I'd appreciate the help, wouldn't you rather be hanging out with your friends?" Greysen asked.

"Polaris is my only friend here." Edwin rubbed behind the old golden retriever's ears, "And they don't let dogs go to school."

She smiled, "Well that sucks. I always thought school would be more fun with animals. How did you want to help?"

Pulling out a folded piece of paper, Edwin turned it around to show Greysen her letter, "You said that for some stars, you can't find the person."

"Yes. Sometimes the coordinates don't show up on the labels. That's what these are," she shifted her bag so that Edwin could see inside.

"What are you doing with them?"

"Hopefully, I'll find out who they belong to."

"How are you going to do that?"

"I'm still working on that part."

"What about letters?"

Greysen caught herself before she could scoff at the idea. She'd considered it, but the hours required to write who knows how many letters and send them off into the ether…

"If you write to the distribution centers with descriptions of the wishes in the stars, you might be able to find their owners."

"That would be a lot of letters," Greysen had specifically stopped counting how many stars were collecting in the watchtower. It was best to have plausible deniability when Cilla asked for a tally of the collection.

"If you have enough help, you wouldn't have to write that many."

"Are you volunteering your summer school class to write letters?"

"It would be more useful than the other stuff we've been learning."

"Well…your teacher and guardian would have to be okay with it."

Edwin shrugged, "I'm sure you grownups can figure that out."

"Alright, I'll have my wife chat with your teacher about it."

"Good. When should I follow up?"

Greysen laughed, "You're very thorough.

How about next week? I think Cilla was going for lunch with your teacher soon."

"Okay," Edwin pet the head of the old golden retriever who seemed to be nudging the boy towards the door.

"Next week then," he said with finality and held out his hand. "It was good to meet you Mrs. Greysen."

"Greysen is just fine. And it was a pleasure to meet you too, Edwin."

The dog pulled at his leash, urging Edwin out of the distribution center. Once he was gone, Greysen shouldered her bag to head out. Slurping his coffee loudly, the manager said, "You shouldn't encourage him."

"In what? Wanting to write some letters?"

"Yes."

"He just wants to help." Greysen shrugged. "So long as his teacher and guardian are okay with it, it seems harmless."

"He'll just be disappointed. You're not gonna find who those stars belong to."

"We won't if we don't try," Greysen replied defiantly. "Even if we only manage to send one of those stars off to their owner, I think it's worth it."

"So long as you're only wasting your own

time."

Greysen stormed out of the office, stalking over to her hover-bike as she grumbled under her breath. Edwin and his dog were only a few yards up the road. It wouldn't hurt to give the kid a ride home. Securing her bag to the rack on her hoverbike, she turned it on and let it coast along until she caught up with him.

"Why don't I give you and your dog a ride home? Would that be okay?"

Edwin looked down at the golden retriever. "Does that sound good Polaris?"

Tail wagging, Polaris licked at Edwin's fingers.

Once her two passengers had helmets secured and Edwin's address was entered into the nav-system, Greysen peeled off across the desert landscape. It didn't take long to arrive at the worn-down farmhouse Edwin called home. He was quick to jump off the hover-bike and help Polaris down before running towards the door.

"I'll get my aunt," he called over his shoulder while Polaris ambled after him.

Greysen made sure her hoverbike was parked in an out-of-the-way spot and waited by the gate for Edwin to reappear with his aunt in tow. Waving, Greysen set down her helmet and offered the other woman a smile. "Sorry for bugging you, just wanted to make sure he made it home."

"I'd wondered where he got off so early this morning." She dried her hands off on her apron, "Thank you for bringing him home…"

"Greysen. I'm a star chaser for the local depot. I think my daughter Eleanor is in his class."

"Ah." recognition dawned, "I'm Narine, it's good to meet you. Edwin, you need to get ready for class.".

"Okay." Narine watched as he started back towards the house.

"I'm sorry about him bugging you at work. I didn't think he was even that interested in the letter."

"It's no trouble, honestly. I was finished up for the night. He said he wanted to help find who the addressless stars belong to. Maybe by writing some letters with his class."

"Oh?"

"He seems pretty enthusiastic about it."

"That would be a nice change. He hasn't been enthusiastic about anything much recently."

"Losing someone is hard on anyone, let alone parents, especially for a kid. Cilla, my wife, has been chatting with his teacher. I was going to ask her to see if maybe these letters could be something Edwin could get credit for in his summer classes."

"That would be lovely. But I don't want to make more work for you."

"It's fine. Besides, it's always worth it to encourage a kid to do something they're interested in before they get bored of it. And maybe it really could help in identifying where some of these stars need to go."

Narine glanced back at the house before saying, "I don't want him to get his hopes up."

"Hope is part of life. We can't avoid it just because it might be disappointing."

"I guess."

"Well," Greysen said as she dug into a pocket, pulling out a card, "I'll talk with my wife, and if you have any questions you can give me a call. Or meet me at the distribution depot, just after daybreak."

Nodding as she looked over Greysen's card she said, "I will. Thank you."

"Of course," Greysen said, hoping that Narine would let Edwin help her.

"How was work, mumma?" Eleanor asked, nearly tackling Greysen as she dropped her gear by the door.

"My shift was great."

"Warren still being sour?" Cilla commented from the kitchen.

"As always," Greysen said as she kicked off her boots, juggling Eleanor in one arm. "But that kid that wrote to me showed up and offered to help figure out who those all belong to." She pointed at the sprawling collection of star cylinders.

Eleanor perked up, "Edwin, right?"

"Yes. He and his dog came to the depot this morning."

"I wish we could have a dog. Mummy there are some that are hyper-allergenic!"

"'Hypo' dear, and no we're not getting a dog," Cilla said firmly, stirring her coffee for a long moment. "Will you let him help?"

"I think so. He wants to write to the other depots with the wish descriptions in case they recognize a local."

"That sounds like a big project for someone Eleanor's age."

Greysen knew when Cilla was trying not to overtly shoot down an idea. "Probably to start, it would just be writing some letters to find out if the other depots have more addressless stars. Maybe help narrow down the general geographical area the star goes to."

"I suppose that's not the worst idea. Though, do you really think the other depots will bother writing back? For all we know, the other depots could be managed by Warren's cousins."

Stifling a laugh, Greysen collapsed on the sofa with Eleanor, "*Stars*, I hope not!"

"It is possible."

"Don't even joke about that!"

"Well, hopefully this means my plants will eventually get their home back," Cilla said. "Ellie-bug, you're going to be late for school. Let's get a move on."

"Okay, okay! I think it would be fun to write letters to the star depots."

"You just want to avoid more math homework."

Their voices faded as Cilla ushered Eleanor upstairs to finish getting ready for the day. Greysen picked up her notebook of stars and flipped to a blank page to start outlining a plan.

In the dark, with wind flipping through her hair was where she felt the most alive. She weaved through the dark shapes of brush, dashing in and around twisted desert trees. A bright explosion above her caught her eye and a rainbow of light streaked across the sky.

She raced ahead, chasing one of the falling stars as it careened towards the horizon, making impact at the base of an old watchtower, its tall shadow breaking the flat landscape. She slowed her hover-bike to a stop near the crater so that she could retrieve it, not expecting to find someone else already at the ledge, looking down at the fallen star.

"Stay back! You don't wanna to get burned by one of those!" She called, grabbing her gear.

The figure turned, illuminated by the afterglow of the star, "I've never seen one up close before."

"Oh?" she peered over the edge, watching the multicolored light as it slowly began to fade.

"I've always wanted to. I've heard they can be incredibly inspiring. But now that it's in front of me, I can't think of how to describe it."

Smiling, she offered, "Magical, maybe?"

The figure smiled back, tucking her hair behind an ear, "That's a start. Have any other good adjectives?"

"Well," she tossed the coolant into the crater before sliding down the edge of it, "Maybe it's easier to describe when you know what it's like to touch one."

"I thought that wasn't allowed?"

"I won't tell anyone if you don't." Putting the cooling rock into a cylinder, she climbed back up the crater to the figure. The coordinates began to appear on the side of the cylinder, and she knew she wouldn't get in trouble, "Besides, I think this one is for you."

The sun was already glaring through the classroom window when Edwin slid into the chair attached to their desk. A few kids not doomed to a summer of extra classes were playing out in the school yard with some kind of flying device. It dipped up and down, colorful streamers trailing behind it against the clear sky before crashing into the ground. The kids had it back up in the air moments later, sending it higher and higher.

"Good morning class. We have a special guest visiting today," the teacher said.

Looping across the window, the flying device zoomed out of Edwin's sight.

"This is Greysen, she's a star chaser. And

also one of Eleanor's moms."

Edwin's attention was pulled back to the front of the classroom. Greysen was decked out in a leather jacket, the arms covered in patches, and a pair of goggles perched in her short curls.

"Thanks for having me."

A hand shot up across the room from Edwin, "My dad said star chasers don't have a bedtime. Is that true?"

Greysen chuckled, "My bedtime is in the morning. Since I'm usually out all night."

"So you're like an owl?" Another student asked.

"Kind of."

"Alright class, we can ask more questions later. For now, I wanted to go over a new project we're going to be working on with Greysen."

"Do we get to go on your hover-bike?"

"Can we stay up for the starfalls?

Their teacher held up a finger to her mouth to ask them all to be quiet, "Questions later. Now remember those letters that we wrote a few weeks ago?"

The class mumbled.

"Well, Edwin wrote an extra letter to Greysen here, and found out that she's been working on stars that don't have a home."

Chairs scraped on the linoleum floor as many of Edwin's classmates turned in their seats to look at them. Edwin sank in their seat, staring at their desk in hopes that the other students would stop staring at them.

"I thought we weren't sending the letters to anyone?"

Greysen interjected, "Well, your teacher is a friend of my wife and asked if Edwin could send his letter to me. And I said yes."

"What do wishing stars have to do with our letters?"

Their teacher smiled, "Edwin had a wonderful idea that maybe we could help Greysen find the owners of the addressless stars by writing letters to different depots to spread the word that Greysen is collecting them in the hopes of finding who they belong to. Hopefully, we can find out if there are more stars needing to find their owners. And then maybe we can help identify locations in the wishes so we can work towards reunification."

"That'll never work," Edwin's neighbor said.

"It could," Edwin replied quietly.

"There are millions of people out there! Even though you can't do math, you should be able to figure out that it's gonna be impossible to find out who they belong to."

"Micah, go sit in the hall for a few minutes," the teacher said, crossing her arms sternly. "We don't insult our classmates."

Rolling his eyes, Micah got up and pushed the door open with a huff before the teacher continued, "We know the chances are slim that we'll be able to find matches for all the stars. But it would be great if we could find some."

"Why don't some of the stars have addresses?" a girl behind Edwin asked.

"They don't know," Edwin said out loud, covering their mouth almost immediately.

Greysen smiled as she replied, "That's right. We don't really know. There are some theories, but none of them have been proven. Sometimes the containers we use just don't have coordinates show up on the label."

"Now class, we're going to split up into teams and each team is going to pick a depot to write to. I'm going to put a list of depots up here on the board. In these letters, I want you to introduce yourselves, detail the project, and ask if anyone at the depot is interested in helping."

There was a tapping on Edwin's shoulder. They turned around to see the girl behind them grinning, "Do you want to be on my team?"

"Uh, sure. I guess."

"Cool, I'm Anya. Is there someone else that you wanted to invite to work with us?"

Shaking their head, Edwin noticed that the other students were quickly splitting off into groups of three and four. Some were crowding around Greysen at the front of the room, peppering her with questions.

"Then would you mind if Ellie joined us?"

Edwin shook their head again.

"Sweet! Ellie! Come sit with us!" the girl called her friend over. She was in a grade above them and always wore the frilliest, fluffiest dresses.

Ellie slid into the seat next to them. "Hey, you're Edwin, right?"

"Uh-huh."

"It's so cool that you wrote to my mumma - this is such a cool idea," Ellie said, pushing a curl behind her ear.

Edwin stared at their feet for a moment, "It wasn't anything special."

"Alright class!" the teacher interjected above the chatter, "Now that you've found your groups, elect a group leader and have them come up to tell me which depot you've decided on. Greysen also has some 'Honorary Star Chaser' badges if anyone would like one."

"Edwin should be our group leader, right Anya?" Ellie said. "He's the reason we're doing the project anyways."

Anya grinned, "Yeah, I vote for Edwin too."

"I've never been a leader before though!" Edwin told them.

"Don't worry about it, you'll be great," Ellie replied. "Which depot should we choose?"

The three of them looked up at the list their teacher had finished writing on the chalkboard. Edwin recognized the name of their hometown, half way down the list. They hadn't been back since moving in with their aunt.

"What about Riverton?" Edwin asked quietly.

After a moment, both girls nodded and Anya said, "Yeah that sounds good. Go tell the teacher, and Ellie and I will start on the first letter."

"Okay," Edwin left their desk to go up to the teacher, "We—Anya, Ellie and me—were wanting to have the depot in Riverton."

The teacher nodded and made a star next to Riverton on the list, "And who is your team leader?"

"Um, they both said I should be."

"That's wonderful Edwin," she said, adding Edwin's name next to the Riverton depot. "You can get started on your letter then."

Greysen held out a couple of the shiny star chaser badges to them with a smile, "Good luck."

Dear Riverton Depot Manager,

we're students taking summer school in Centerville and are writing to you in hopes that we might be able to match some wishing stars our local star chaser (she's one of Ellie's moms) has been holding onto. She's found a bunch of stars that don't have coordinates, so there's no way to send them off to who they belong to. Can we send you a copy of her notes on the wishes and dreams for each star to see if any might be a match to anyone in your area?

Also, if your depot has any stars without an address, you can send us notes about the wishes and we'll try to match them to people here in Centerville, or pass them on to our classmates.

Thank you,
Please write back!

- Edwin, Anya and Ellie
P.S. Edwin used to live in Riverton!

Edwin, Anya and Ellie,

Thank you for writing to us about your project. We've heard about some depots collecting stars with no coordinates, so it's wonderful to know that y'all are working to get them off to where they belong. I don't know if we have the staff to help with your project. But I can make some calls for volunteers. Please, go ahead and send over those notes and we'll see what we can do.

We do have a handful of stars without coordinates ourselves, so I'll see if any of our chasers can get some notes written up on those *for you.*

    Also great to hear that you're from here Edwin. Stop in anytime you visit and ask for me.

Good Luck Kids,
- Burton Rogers, Riverton Depot Manager

Leaning back against a large, flat rock, Greysen yawned.

"Don'tcha start that nonsense already. It's only midnight," Marie chastised.

"Sorry, I've been staying up late helping the summer school kids with their letters. I'm wiped."

"It's already been a year? Two? You still have stars needin' homes?"

Greysen nodded, stifling another yawn, "Just short of two years now. The kids are pretty good at connecting with different depots. They've even gotten other schools involved to help with the workload. And with more depots, we keep finding more way-ward stars. We even have ones being sent to us from the other side of the world that we're helping to identify."

Marie chuckled, "Well, I never expected that one little canister would turn into such a big thing. No wonder Cilla hasn't been making my favorites lately."

"Eh, she's on deadline right now so she's stressed about that. And having stars strewn all around the house isn't helping."

"When's her deadline up? I'm planning a bit of a get together."

"I think at the end of the month. And what kind of get together?"

"The retirement kind."

Greysen shot up right, "You're retiring?"

"It's about time I am. I want to go spend my days at the beach with my grandkids."

"But you've been a chaser forever–"

"Only fifty years. Started when I was but a young lass and still had both legs," she cackled and began lighting up a cigarette. "Besides, your generation will do just fine with the stars. I mean you've managed to get more stars home to their owners than most chasers in this district."

"I can't take credit for most of that. It's been the kids writing all those letters. Edwin has been working on creating the database to store and sort all the information."

"Hrm, sounds like a pretty smart kid."

"He is. I think he'll probably do well at whatever he decides to do."

Marie chuckled, "I'm sure you'd like for him to go into star chasing since Eleanor wasn't interested in that."

"I mean, if he wants to," Greysen replied with a shrug. "I know not everyone gets how amazing this job is. Everyone seems to be more preoccupied with getting their own star rather than the gift it is to give someone theirs."

"Have you ever gotten a star, Greysen?"

She'd had a few over the years. But the one that mattered, that sent her off on her current journey, was the one she always thought of. "Yeah, I have."

"And what was in that star?"

"It was me catching a star. I went and applied to be a star chaser that day."

Marie raised a knowing eyebrow, "*Only* a star?"

"Okay, well, Cilla was there. But I didn't know it was Cilla at the time. Just that I'd chase a star one day and meet the most beautiful woman ever."

"We're all inspired to do things differently. You started chasing stars so you might find the girl of your dreams. But this is just a job to me. And it's time to have some me-time, for my own dreams."

"I'll miss you."

"You just need to look up and think of me and you'll hear my cranky old voice reminding you to let the wind whip through your hair."

Greysen turned her gaze upward at the speckled navy blanket above. A few of the stars winked knowingly, and the whisper of a breeze carried the gentle quiet of the desert. She didn't understand how anyone could trade this for something else. Especially a sandy, smelly beach. But like Marie had said, to some it was just a job. A way to spend the time and earn a living.

A bright streak of a star falling crossed the sky above them and in the background their radios cackled to life.

She only hoped that one of her last nights on the job would be a beautiful star storm.

Edwin wasn't used to being alone around so many adults. Sure Narine had just stepped away to grab something to drink, but it all reminded them of the wake. All their parents' friends had been dressed in dark colors that must have been hidden away in their closets. They'd been told every version of *sorry*. And hugged. And cried on. And told to be brave. And that things would be better again soon. The whole experience had been suffocating. Even several years later, it wasn't something that Edwin wanted to repeat anytime soon.

This was a party though. A celebration of one of Greysen's co-workers retiring. Edwin had only met her once when Greysen had brought her along to talk to the summer school class. Old people were confusing. Why invite a bunch of kids you didn't really know to a retirement party?

But it had been an excuse to wear the frilly skirt that Ellie had given them though. She'd been going through a growth spurt and it was too short for her now and Ellie knew how much Edwin had admired the little bunnies on the lace trim. With their darker hair growing longer, Edwin was feeling a bit more themself and more pretty.

The general hubbub was interrupted by a spoon clinking against a glass for everyone's attention.

"Quiet, quiet everyone!" Marie called out

from the middle of the crowded patio. "I'm glad you all made time for this."

There was a cheer from the party goers. "You all owe the Riverton Depot some drinks for covering our routes for the night," Marie continued. "Now, I'm not gonna make a long speech or anything. None of us are gonna live long enough to care. So, enjoy the booze and the food, and don't you dare touch those ginger cookies that Cilla made. Those are mine. Cheers!"

In the midst of laughter and applause, a tap on their shoulder got Edwin's attention.

"That skirt looks so good on you," Ellie gushed.

Edwin felt their cheeks grow hot. "I didn't know if you were going to come."

"Of course! I love parties. And I would never miss one of Marie's. They're legendary at the depot."

"You two should get some drinks and snacks before they're all gone," Narine told them, returning from finding the drink table.

Ellie brandished her wide smile and grabbed Edwin's hand, pulling them along through the crowd. "There's supposed to be a really amazing star shower later tonight. Do you think your aunt will let you stay up?"

"I dunno. It's supposed to be pretty late, isn't it?"

"2 AM or something," Ellie replied, surveying the lemonade options.

"I can ask."

"Okay. My moms said we could watch it from the roof if it's alright with your aunt. It's not like we have class tomorrow."

"That sounds like fun."

"Good. I wish we didn't have to do so much extra school during the summer. I'd much rather go to camp or something."

"Are there camps out here?" Edwin asked.

"No. Not really. But in the movies, a lot of people just take a bus to a camp somewhere in the woods."

"Those are just movies though."

"Yeah, I guess," Ellie lamented. "Oh! Remember that one star with the wish about going traveling that we were having a really hard time figuring out where to write to about?"

"Yeah…"

"I was thinking we should try the European depots. Some of the street descriptions sound like maybe they might be somewhere there."

"Would a star from that far away really

land all the way out here?"

"Sure is - mumma had a star last winter from a little village in Eastern Europe. Anything is possible. Besides, if it was easy to get them to the right person then we wouldn't have become friends."

"That's true," Edwin said, loading up a paper plate with a hotdog and chips before following Ellie off to the low stone wall that surrounded the little patio.

They kicked their feet back and forth as they ate, pointing out constellations and planets and passing satellites that blinked across the sky.

"I have some more dresses and skirts I can give you if you want," Ellie told Edwin. "Mummy said it's okay since they don't fit anymore."

"I don't know if I'd wear them enough."

Ellie shrugged, "Well no one else is gonna wear them. You can try them on tonight."

"Okay."

Ellie's parents eventually found them at the edge of the party and Cilla asked them, "What kind of mischief are you planning over here?"

"Just where to send the next batch of letters."

Cilla shook her head, "You're just as bad as Greysen. All you think about is those stars."

"It clearly runs in the family," Greysen said. "Are you coming over tonight Edwin?"

"Um, I still need to ask my aunt. But thank you for inviting me."

"Of course. You're always welcome to stay over."

Both of them clamored up the stairs to Ellie's room, kicking off their shoes before collapsing on her bed.

"Not so loud you two," Cilla called after them. But they were already giggling from too many popsicles.

"Let's do a fashion show," Ellie suggested, getting up to open the door to her wardrobe. "That way we can be dressed in style for the star shower."

Edwin twined their fingers in the fabric of their skirt, "You're sure?"

"Of course. You can try on anything you want."

An array of brightly colored dresses and skirts bulged out of the wardrobe as Ellie pulled it open. She began pulling out a few, holding them up to herself in the mirror before moving on to the next. Edwin slid off the bed and joined her, gently running their hands over the garments. A spray of sequins on one skirt reminded them of a dark blue dress their mom had worn. The sequins twinkled like stars when she wore it, and made her look like an old movie star.

Pausing on a soft pink sundress, Edwin turned to Ellie, "Can I try on this one?"

Ellie pulled it off the hanger and handed it to Edwin, "Sure. The bathroom is next door, remember?"

Clutching the dress tightly, Edwin retreated to the bathroom with it. Taking off their shirt, Edwin pulled the dress over their shoulders and pulled off their skirt. The dress was lightweight and flowy, not restrictive like the shorts they were used to wearing in the summer. They twirled a few times and caught themselves smiling in the mirror.

If only their hair were long enough to braid or do anything with they would almost look like a girl.

They knocked on Ellie's door, waiting for her to tell them to come in, their arms full of their other clothes.

"Oh, I think pink is definitely your color,

Edwin. It brings out your cheeks," Ellie said. She had put on a green sun dress that matched the one Edwin was wearing. "I've decided that I want us to match, if that's okay?"

Edwin nodded and set down their clothes, twisting their hips back and forth so that the dress swished, "I really like this one."

"Good, you can have it! I have a couple of other pink ones you can try on too."

"Maybe later. We don't want to miss the star shower."

As if on cue, Ellie produced rolled-up blankets and an armful of pillows for them, "I'm all set."

With a nest of blankets set up on the rooftop balcony, the two of them laid down watching the sky. The sugar rush was beginning to wear off and Edwin was having a hard time keeping their eyes open.

"Edwin, I'm really glad I can be myself with you."

"Oh?"

"Yeah. A lot of people don't like girls that are loud."

"Girls can't be loud?"

"According to some people. Mostly dumb boys."

"Boys are pretty dumb," Edwin agreed.

"Not you though."

"I don't know if I'm a boy."

"Then definitely not you."

Edwin smiled to themself. It was nice not to be grouped in with the boys.

"Are you a girl then?"

Edwin blinked at Ellie, "Maybe?"

"Well, my moms say that you don't have to know that sort of thing yet, if ever. People are supposed to have time to figure it all that out for themselves."

"Really?"

"Uh huh. Like, I think I like girls. But even if that changes, it's okay."

"Oh, that makes sense. So you want a wife, like your moms?"

Ellie yawned, "Maybe someday. Having a wife that can bake like mummy can would be cool. I suck at cooking."

Edwin giggled, "You really do!"

"Hey! It's not my fault– the directions for that pizza were wrong!"

"I thought we were going to be in so much trouble with Cilla."

"I mean, we didn't burn the watchtower down."

"Barely. I definitely think you need a wife. Or someone that can cook much better than you so you don't starve."

"I won't starve-that's what takeout is for!"

A star streaked across the sky, "You'd better make a wish for it then."

Sitting in the cold clinic chair and waiting was the worst kind of torture to be put through. Every time she heard footsteps, she expected the door to open. But it didn't. Had they lost the test results? Or were they just unsure? She hated having to be there alone. But it didn't make sense for both of them to miss work she supposed. Especially not so early on.

The door finally opened, and the doctor slipped on their glasses as they came into the room. "How are you doing today?"

"Good."

Nodding, the doctor shuffled through a folder before pulling out a piece of paper.

"Nervous, I guess."

"That's perfectly normal. Especially for a new parent-to-be."

It took her a moment to process. "I'm-"

"You're pregnant."
Relief. Excitement. Worry. Panic.
"I'm going to be a mom?"
"Yes, congratulations."

"Edwina!" Ellie didn't bother knocking before bursting into Edwina's room, her hands cupping something. "I couldn't wait to show you!"

Edwina pulled off her headphones, and shifted her white cat aside so Ellie could sit on the corner of the bed, "What?"

Luna protested by trying to bite the cord of Edwina's headphones.

Her friend's excitement was practically making her vibrate, "I finally got a star!"

Edwina smiled quickly to hide her own disappointment. They'd been making wishes together for years now, promising that they would immediately share it with each other when they got their first one.

"That's great! What's the wish?"

Ellie turned the star over a few times in her hands, "You should see for yourself."

"What? No, I couldn't–"

"Come on Edwina. You're the only one I want to share my wishes with. Please?" Ellie held out the star, which sparkled as it caught the light.

Biting her lip, Edwina reached forward and brushed her fingers over the surface.

She was shivering, and drenched. The white box of pastries smashed on the pavement in front of her.

She'd held her mom's star so many times, but it was still strange touching someone else's wishing star. The foreign emotions were much stronger than from her mom's star. Probably because Ellie's was much newer.

Ellie looked at her hopefully, "Well?"

"I only got a part of it. Just a minute," Edwina assured her friend, wrapping her hand around the star.

Even though she was shivering, she was hot with rage. What kind of idiot wouldn't look where they were walking? As she got to her feet, she rounded on the stranger only to be met with a mousy-looking girl on the verge of a panic attack.

Taking a deep breath, Ellie glanced at her ruined pastries. It was just a box of delicious treats. They could be replaced. It wasn't the end of the world.

"Try to watch out for people," she chastised, only for the girl to burst into tears.

"I'm sorry! I was rushing and didn't see you. And I managed to get lost and—"

"Whoa, hold on. It's fine. Besides, we're both soaked. So we're even I guess."

Sniffling, the girl shook her head, "I'm never going to make it to my interview now. And that means I'm never going to get into this program. And I'll never get my degree, and I'll end up having to move back home..."

"Don't get ahead of yourself. Just call them and say you're running late. If anything, it will be a good story for your interview."

She hiccupped, "You think so?"

Looking around, she spotted a cafe across the street, "For the moment though, let's get dried off."

The mousy girl smiled and she could feel her heart melt. And flutter. And this must feel like what falling stars feel. The rush of not being able to breathe, and falling faster and faster.

Edwina pulled her hand away, heart pounding, "That's..."

"Romantic? Right?" Ellie fell back onto the bed, nearly missing Luna. "It's so classic lesbian too, isn't it? Girl meets girl. Girl asks girl out for coffee. Girl falls in love with girl."

"All that's missing is the moving truck."

"Shush you!"

"No, it's a good one."

"Ugh, I can't wait to fall in love. I hope she's gorgeous, just like in my dream. And loves singing at the top of her lungs with me."

"Falling in love is tricky. And messy."

"That's the best part! And besides, we'll have each other for all the messy parts."

"But you graduate this year. You're going to go off and make college friends," Edwina pulled Luna into her lap for comfort.

Ellie gave her a goofy smile, "I am not going to abandon my best friend just because I'm going off to college at the end of the year. Besides, we're two of the best letter writers around." She pointed at the framed plaque across the room, "That award says so!"

Holding out her pinky to Ellie, Edwina asked, "Pinky swear? That we'll stay friends?"

"And cohorts in mischief and letter writing, forever!" Ellie linked her pinky with Edwina's.

"Besides, I know you'll get your wish soon. For someone tall, dark and handsome."

"Maybe…"

"You will! I have a feeling."

Edwina shook her head, "Your 'feelings' mean nothing."

"I predicted you'd get Luna."

"You guessed that we'd adopt another pet after Polaris died."

"I knew it would be a cat."

"You already knew that Auntie Narine prefers cats."

"Well I still have a feeling. And we'll make more wishes at star fall this weekend. Okay? I need my best friend to have someone to take care of them. And some one for my dream girl to bake cookies for."

"You are ridiculous. And also the best friend I could have asked for."

"I know. Oh, we also need to make some wishes that I'll get that scholarship. Not all of us are whizzes like you."

"I'm not a whiz…"

"You're not even starting college for another year and you already have offers for a place in half a dozen magical engineering programs."

Edwina shrugged, "I'm still hoping to get into the same school as you."

"You will. They're just trying to come up with a scholarship offer you can't refuse."

"How are you so optimistic all the time?"

"It's one of my great faults. Along with my good looks and fashion sense. What did you want to do this afternoon by the way?"

"Oh, I promised to help your mom with some more letters."

Ellie giggled, "Good. I think mummy is about ready to kill mumma over the stars that are spread out all over the kitchen again."

"We are a little behind."

"Don't tell mummy that. You could come over for dinner this weekend? Mumma doesn't have work on Friday night. So we could work on some letters, and then you could sleep over."

"Alright. I'll let my aunt know."

The star project had evolved into slightly more organized chaos. Edwina spent hours of her free time programming and inputting data into custom databases. They'd come up with a lot of interesting patterns and findings, especially in the last couple of years. Hopefully, all that work would help Edwina get into her dream school.

Greysen dropped a crate with the latest batch of letters on the table, "Well, this is all from this month."

Edwina frowned and leaned over to

thumb through them, "That's a lot. We don't even have this many missing stars anymore."

"Most probably need to be rerouted to other depots."

"Hopefully I'll have some of the automation worked out before school starts."

Ellie set down a plate of freshly baked cookies, "Yeah, you'll have too much school work otherwise."

"I mean, I can still make time to help. Especially while we work out the kinks in the automation."

"Don't stress about it, kiddo. If you have to focus on school, that's fine."

"Hey, hun?" Cilla called from the kitchen, "What about these cylinders up here?"

There were a handful of dusty cylinders stuffed on the top cabinets in the kitchen that they had yet to identify.

"We're still working on those ones I think Cilla," Edwina replied.

"Can they be relocated somewhere else? My pothos clippings are beginning to overrun their current spot."

Greysen got up and retrieved the cylinders, noting the blue star on the lid of one of them.

"That's an old one," Edwina said, looking at the date.

"Yeah. It was one of my first addressless ones."

"But we haven't identified who it goes to yet?"

Shaking her head, Greysen pulled up the database entry for it, "No. I narrowed down the location in the dream. But other than that, I'm stuck."

"What's the location?" Ellie asked.

"Riverton. I think," Greysen said, snagging a cookie.

"That should be easy then. It's so close."

"There are still hundreds of thousands of possible owners," Edwina said.

"Have we written to Riverton about it recently?"

Greysen checked the notes in the database, "Not recently. The last time was over five years ago."

"I'll add it to our follow-up list then," Edwina said, typing out a note.

He wasn't sure why he was still nervous when he saw the dark-haired girl on the train. They'd spoken a few times now. So he hoped she wasn't bothered by his attempts at small talk. But every time he spotted her pink cat-eared headphones, his chest got tight and his mind went blank. She was sitting next to another girl that day, and they were chatting and looking at each other's phones as the train rumbled along.

The girl looked up and spotted him standing at the other end of the train car. She blushed and quickly turned back to her friend. Were they talking about him? Or had they just gone back to their conversation? He hoped she was talking about him. Maybe imagining a date they might go on. Was that weird? It had to be weird. Besides, she was probably taken. Someone with a smile that could light you up from the inside out had to already be in love with someone else.

As the train lurched to a stop at another station, the isle cleared, leaving a path to the girl and her friend. Those few words they'd exchanged a few weeks ago 'I like your headphones' and 'Thanks', had been living in his head all this time. He could do better than just an awkward compliment. But that required talking to her again. And this time, in front of someone else.

A couple of people boarded the train, and his feet started moving before he could think. He should have planned something to say. Instead, he stopped next to her seat and she looked up at him.

"Um...hi." She was going to think he was an idiot. "Again."

She tucked a strand of dark hair behind her ear and her friend nudged her, "Hi."

"Do you go to school nearby?" That was definitely too personal to ask a stranger.

Nodding, her friend leaned over her, "Do you?"

"Yeah. I'm a magical engineering student. I specialize in star research."

The friend's smile widened, "So does she. Are you going to the department mixer?"

"Those aren't really my thing," he said. Why wasn't she talking? Was she not interested? Or maybe just shy?

"Well, we'll be there," the friend replied with a shrug. "Oh look, this is our stop."

The two girls got up and squeezed by him to leave the train compartment. They were whispering hurriedly to each other while he stared after them. His brain was trying to figure out if he'd just been asked out in a roundabout way. As the doors began closing he realized it was also his stop. Running after the two girls, he made it off the train but didn't see them on the platform.

He'd have to look for her at that mixer. He'd have to figure out what to wear. And how to ask her out on a proper date.

Pulling down an old cylinder from its shelf, Greysen wiped the dust from the glass as she walked over to the little seating area. The little blue star next to the collection date had nearly faded away.

Cilla glanced up from her book with a curious look, "Did you get another star identified?"

"I think so."

"That's a pretty old one, isn't it?"

"It was one we were having problems with."

"Well, that's good—you finally found out who it belongs to! Where are you sending it?"

Deactivating the cylinder, Greysen opened a small, wooden box and shook the star into it. "I'm packing it up for Edwina."

"It's Edwina's–?"

Greysen wasn't surprised at Cilla's

confusion, "I didn't realize it until recently. But, yeah."

"You've had it for years though."

"She wasn't ready for it yet," Greysen tied the box up with a purple ribbon and set it aside for when they'd sent her off the next day.

Another summer had nearly gone, making eight since Edwina had written that fateful first letter. She was nervously excited to be leaving the little desert town that had been home for almost a decade. But Ellie was going to pick her up from the station once she reached the city and help show her around.

Cilla held out a bag filled with cookies and pulled Edwina into a hug. "When you run out of these, just give us a call and I'll mail you some more. I made sure to make some lemon cookies for Ellie too so don't be guilted into giving up yours."

"You didn't have to do that Cilla," Edwina said.

"Home baked goods go a long way to happy roommate situations," her aunt Narine said.

"Alright, thank you."

Greysen pulled Edwina into a hug next, "I'm gonna miss you."

"And all my help with the star project?"

"Well yes, but mostly you." Greysen handed Edwina a small package, an unfamiliar expression on her face, "Wait 'til you're on the train to open it."

"Why can't I open it now?"

"Cause then I might cry," Greysen's eyes were already shining with tears.

The train horn blared and an announcement on the platform proclaimed that the train would be leaving in two minutes.

Edwina quickly pulled Narine into a tight hug, "I'll call when I get there."

"I know. Just take care of yourself, sweetie. You're going to do great."

"Thanks. I'll see you all for winter break?"

"Of course. Now get on the train before it leaves without you!" Narine called after her.

Grinning, Edwina raced to the carriage door and took the steps two at a time as the conductor blew their whistle. She double-checked her seat number and raced to her seat, pulling down the window to wave goodbye as the train lurched forward.

"Good luck!" Cilla, Greysen, and Aunt Narine called out.

As the platform faded into the distance, Edwina settled into her seat and put on her pink, cat ear headphones. She dug the gift from Greysen from her brown leather purse and pulled at the purple ribbon. Under the wrapping, it was a plain wooden box, like the ones they'd used to ship stars to various depots. And it was heavy enough to be a star.

Sure enough, a metallic, gray rock sat inside under a note from Greysen, *'This has been waiting for you.'*

For a long moment, Edwina just stared at it. She hadn't thought that she'd get a wish. Especially not one from Greysen. Running a finger over the smooth surface, her heart fluttered.

A heart had been traced into the condensation on a window as trees and houses whipped past. The train car swayed gently, rumbling as it crossed streets, a distant sound of the crossing bells ringing penetrating the hum of music through headphones.

Edwina took a deep breath, "It's finally me…"

ABOUT THE AUTHOR

Cay Fletcher is a Queer author with a passion for fantasy and science fiction. Crafting rich landscapes and memorable characters in new and exciting worlds.

Living in the Portland metro area, Cay spends their free time in the garden, cooking, or making a mess, aka crafting. She spent over fifteen years volunteering at fan conventions across the US and still occasionally assists at events in the PNW. As a writer, Cay strives to create relatable queer characters, giving them the titles of hero and protagonist.

They also love to use their crafting and graphic design skills to make products such as patchwork book sleeves, TTRPG journals, stickers, bookmarks, and more. She lives with their wife Sam, their roommate, and their tuxedo cat Satsuki.

Cay uses She/They pronouns.

You can connect with Cay on social media or Goodreads.

www.cayfletcher.com

@cayfletcher

NEWSLETTER

Want to be the first to get the news?

Stay up to date with new releases by subscribing to my newsletter.

www.cayfletcher.com/newsletter

ACKNOWLEDGEMENTS

Huge thank you to my Beta Readers:

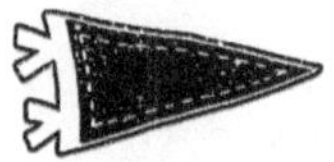

Mel, Naomi, Muse, JC, Jillian, Rachel & Heidi

To my Wife and Roommate for constantly cheering
me on throughout my writing journey.

The Scribbler's Club and Ann for helping me buckle
down and get the work done.

And to Cierra & their team at Spoke and Word Books,
Rafael and John of Always Here Bookstore, and the
formidable Kel for all being champions of queer, indie
books!